Buzz

A Novella

S.L. Freeman

Buzz

ISBN No. 978-0-6151-8397-8

For my immediate and extended family

People pay for what they do, and still more for what they have allowed themselves to become. And they pay for it very simply; by the lives they lead.

James Baldwin (1924-1987)

Daniel Smith stood up from his leather recliner and politely dismissed Edmund, his personal assistant of 22 years, for the day. It was the first time Daniel had ever done that. Edmund was stunned, because he now had nothing to do for the remaining five hours of a workday for the first time in three decades. Edmund knew Daniel almost better than he knew himself and noticed an ever-so-slight quiver of Daniel's upper lip. But, afraid of the answer that may come if he inquired about the apparent problem, Edmund simply accepted his early release and quietly shuffled off to prepare to leave. Daniel, who hadn't taken a step when he rose from the chair, sat back down and stared into the dormant fireplace next to him, a lone tear dropping from his cheek past his silk robe and onto his newspaper.

Chapter 1

Nobody was completely certain about its origins, but the central Montana town of Rossage was presumably named for its first mayor, John Ross, and for the constant sagebrush that would blow through the dirt streets in the late 1800s when it was founded. Rossage now has 20,000 residents. When Daniel Smith founded Apache Foods there in 1973, the population was 1,000. Rossage is Apache Foods, and Apache Foods is Rossage.

Apache Foods sits on 20 acres of tree-lined farmland in the western half of Vilanova County. Since it was founded, the company has provided a vast array of mostly sweet edibles and carved for itself a multi-million-dollar niche, primarily in the Mountain Time zone. People won't hear much about Apache's offerings if they live in the big cities, other than maybe Denver or Omaha; but they might have eaten one of the companies' 25-cent snack cakes or mini bags of potato chips from a convenience store after a hunger-inducing night out. This may not have been quite what Daniel Smith had imagined back in '73, but he didn't mind the additional $300,000 in annual revenue that came in from eastern seaboard cities such as Miami, New York, and Philadelphia. Smith, a full-blooded Apache Indian, is the chief executive officer of the company, and it was through plenty of ups and downs that his dream materialized.

Daniel grew up in the 1950s on a Montana reservation. His parents, Anna and Arthur, were of the Lipan Apaches in Texas and had moved to Montana with baby Daniel after visiting Blackfeet relatives and never going back home. Arthur worked as a carpenter and Anna was a housewife and part-time seamstress. Their surname was given to them by the government office in the state capital, Helena, because they didn't have proof of their given name on paper. Daniel was considered by the people around him to be very mature and kindhearted. His grandmother called him a 'giving soul' when the local paper did its annual Indian Roundup stories that often inflamed tensions in the community by their very title. But 'tough minded' and 'purposeful' were other adjectives used in the articles to describe Daniel, who also earned respect as a member of the football team at Rossage High School. The reservation the family lived on sat right on the outskirts of the town where the company now generates millions. But Apache Foods wasn't founded without a fight.

In 1973, as in many years before and after, it wasn't a simple process for an Indian to start his own business, let alone have a happy existence in town. While there weren't daily outbursts of violence or constant crank calls, Smith endured the occasional taunt, often in the form of bartenders at the local watering hole giving him the wary look when he ordered a drink, or the occasional casino joke. It was usually from someone who knew he was trying to get a business up and running in what they considered to be 'their town.' A few small protests occurred, but nothing violent ever ensued. The tension, however, settled down once it was apparent that nothing could be done to prevent the business from being founded. One time, at Chandler's Hardware Store, a white man in line standing behind Daniel and his mother whispered "you little red nigger" to him. Daniel had no idea what that meant at the time, but the moment stayed with him forever. One of his regrets to this day had been that he hadn't founded the company in a more populated and diverse area, so that his company could also be more diverse.

Daniel always had a talent for baking. Anna raised Daniel alone after he turned 8 – his father had died of a heart attack – and would always give him time on Sundays to perfect his beloved craft, especially since the cakes he made were so good. He would bake his cinnamon- and chocolate-based cakes, carved into 3-inch circular shapes and frosted with his mom's chocolate or vanilla icing, get his bicycle, and go door-to-door, selling them for a dime apiece. Indians got a nickel discount. Some of the residents in town who knew his parents would oblige him, buying one or two, and the hardware store owner, Howard Chandler, made sure to get a dollar's worth every Sunday evening. However, some white youths would bother Daniel from time to time, steal his cakes, or even buy some and then laugh while telling him not to spend the money on liquor. Smith was hurt by the insults, but Anna never let him stray from his focus of bettering himself. Daniel became a model student at Rossage High and then at the University of Montana, where he graduated with a bachelor's degree in economics. He had also minored in food studies, and this background (and there being no bakeries in town) allowed him to pursue his dream of starting his own business.

Daniel was incredibly nervous on a cold winter day in 1972 when he entered the hardware store. Howard Chandler had known his parents well and was always good to him, but an Indian never fully knew what to expect from a white man. It turned out that Howard wasn't there, gone to pick up some tools to sell from a manufacturer several hours away. His son, Edmund, was there to tend shop. Edmund and Daniel were the same age, and Edmund had been one of the people who befriended Daniel over the early years. Edmund was very intelligent but also extremely soft-spoken, not one to 'rock the boat' or even ask many questions. But he was reliable and good with numbers. He had just graduated from the University of Chicago with a statistics degree and was pondering whether to leave his father and the hardware store business and go back to Chicago to begin a new life. But after only an hour of chat with Daniel over a soda in the back of the store, the two decided to ask Howard for help getting started, and Apache Foods was born.

There was no problem with the name of the company. Edmund, who would be chief financial officer, had been a tireless advocate behind the scenes for minority rights in Chicago during his college years and was honored that the company would have that name. He knew firsthand what Daniel had been through, though he never could muster the courage to help his friend through many of the episodes. Maybe now, he thought, he could pay Daniel back by helping him earn enough to keep the business afloat. By 1997, the two had steered the bakery from a small business in a sleepy town to a major Montana company with sales to 35 of the 50 American states and annual revenues of more than $40 million. They were responsible for hiring 2,000 local employees and pumping life into Rossage, making it a hub for truckers to stop for rest and a meal on the interstate that ran through town on its way toward Seattle. And they helped several families to become solvent enough to own their own homes and put kids through school. Even the hardened bigots who had grown up taunting Daniel put their prejudices aside as the company built civic pride in a town they grew up wanting to escape from to greener pastures. The employees were a cohesive bunch, working mainly in distribution and on the assembly line for the millions of cakes, pies, and salty snacks Apache would send to store shelves each year. And there had never been a major accident or complaint that needed a courtroom to settle. Daniel, now 54, and his 86-year-old mother had a good life and had earned the respect of everyone; everyone except for Greg Farber.

Chapter 2

Rossage High School wasn't huge, but it wasn't small either. With about 3,000 students, it served a few communities in the area, and, as such, had a pretty good athletic program. As is the case in many rural small towns, football was king in Rossage, and during many seasons, the team was almost guaranteed to make the playoffs and compete for the Montana state championship. Daniel was a good athlete, which made him a good football player, too. He played wide receiver and used football as a way to help form bonds with many of the students that he didn't speak much to off the field, or, rather, those students who didn't speak much to him off the field. Like his father, Daniel's idol was the great Jim Thorpe, who meant everything athletically and socially to Native Americans. For Daniel, Thorpe was especially inspirational. Arthur had kept an autographed photo of Thorpe in the master bedroom.

Daniel helped lead his team, the Cardinals, to the district playoffs in his senior year of 1967. The Cardinals, who had an 8-2 record that season, played Madison High School, from about 15 miles down the interstate. The Beavers were undefeated, at 10-0, and were favored to win the state title.

The game was played on a rainy Friday night in Helena. The muddy conditions and raucous crowd made for a great atmosphere, and the players on both sides felt the pressure to win. A scoreless tie remained through three quarters, and with only a few seconds left in the final period, the Rossage quarterback lobbed a pass toward the corner of the end zone. Daniel Smith was the intended target.

Chapter 3

Greg Farber had it tough in life. His father, Hank, was abusive and an alcoholic. He treated Greg and his mother, Jean, poorly most of the time, which translated into plenty of sleepless nights for Greg worrying about his mother and himself. Hank didn't have an excuse for his behavior, but if one wanted to find a reason for it, they could start by trying to pin his bad acts on his work life. Hank had been in and out of the already-scarce Madison job market for several years now. A self-taught mechanic, he also had odd jobs as a painter and carpenter. He had trouble providing for the family consistently and it caused him to escape through the bottle. His frustration peaked when he lost a chance at a more-lucrative opportunity to be a corrections officer at the Bryan State Prison, about 20 miles north of Madison.

Hank had arrived on time for the interview and had a referral from a friend who had already been working in the system. He was certain that he would get the job, be able to make his family happier, and stop himself from drinking so much. He didn't get the job. It was a crushing blow. When he received the fateful call, he lashed out at the secretary whose job it was to give him the bad news, asking repeatedly – and loudly – for the name of the person who got the job before slamming the phone down in frustration. Of course, the secretary wouldn't tell him. But the connected friend who had referred him had the inside information. The bigwigs at the prison liked the toughness and attitude of the other job applicant so much that even a bona fide referral wasn't enough to save Hank. The person who was hired instead was Arthur Smith. Incensed that an Indian was offered the spot, Hank degraded Native Americans so much from that point forward that it was nearly impossible for Greg not to feel somewhat the same as his dad, seeing as though he was too young yet to understand that the hiring process in Hank's case had been fairly done. All Greg did was see his father angry, be told over and over that it was an Indian's fault, and watch his mother suffer the consequences. Greg eventually hated his father; but he hated Indians even more, ultimately blaming them for his situation.

Greg grew to be lean and svelte at 5-foot, 11-inches, a perfect size for a defensive back in football. He made the all-state team at Madison High and signed a football scholarship with the University of Montana. In the final seconds of his last high school game in 1967, Greg looked high in the air to see a football coming slowly his way. Also racing toward him was the wide receiver for Rossage, Daniel Smith. Greg had him played perfectly and was thinking to himself that this play was not only going to end his high school football career but also exorcise some longstanding personal demons. He would get revenge for Hank, who was watching nervously in the stands, against the dreaded Indian's son. It wouldn't be much, but it would be something. Maybe then the abuse would end.

As the ball floated, two lives would intersect and be changed forever. Daniel faked to the inside, and Greg stopped suddenly to try to change direction with him. Greg's foot got caught in the grass in a small divot, twisting his knee while his foot stayed put. He couldn't jump; but Daniel could, leaping to make the catch. It was the game-winning touchdown as time expired. The scoreboard read Rossage 6, Madison 0. As Daniel's teammates mobbed him in the end zone celebrating, Greg lay on the ground writhing in pain as Hank's head looked straight down in the stands. Daniel, despite all the attention, worked his way through the crowd to find out if Greg was OK. Greg waved him off in disgust and was then immediately carried off on a stretcher, his knee wrecked. A week later, the University of Montana rescinded his scholarship offer. In Hank's mind, even though Arthur Smith had passed away years prior, it was another indignity at the hands of a Smith, an Indian. He took it out on Greg and Jean, relentlessly, until he succumbed to his own self-induced stress, dying of heart failure three years later. During that time, Greg had reached the pinnacle of anger, frustration, sorrow, and pain.

Chapter 4

Daniel and Edmund, the founding fathers of Apache Foods, were known throughout the region for being fair and honest employers. They were willing to hire anyone who could show that they would be loyal and hardworking, whether they were driving trucks, on the assembly line, or in a cubicle. Despite turning themselves into VIPs, Daniel or Edmund made an attempt to sit in on almost every interview of a finalist for any opening. They wanted to show potential workers that they weren't the type to sit in the office on high and look down upon them. Apache workers appreciated this attitude from their superiors, and good relations were fostered company-wide.

On June 10, 1999, a prospective employee walked into the main offices of Apache, dressed in a navy polyester suit and carrying a briefcase that had shown signs of wear and tear. As it was, Edmund was in the human resources office that day discussing some new procedures with the generalists. When the large oak door gently opened, Edmund stopped talking in mid-sentence and looked up with a surprised but pleased look. Standing before him in the polyester suit and holding the natty briefcase was Greg Farber.

Greg had come a long way since that night in high school 32 years ago, Edmund thought, remembering how he had seen Greg give Daniel the cold shoulder from the stands after the final play of the big game. Now, all these years later, Greg had arrived at the biggest company in the state to let bygones be bygones. Edmund greeted Greg and, of course, went through the customary reminiscing that most people go through when they see an old high school rival or classmate. Greg smiled appreciatively and mentioned that he had managed to rehabilitate his knee enough to earn a Division III scholarship at a small school in North Dakota but that he passed it up and became a mechanic, like his father. He looked down as he spoke, as he still sported a tiny bit of shame and regret at his decision not to leave the abusive household he was a part of all those years ago. But now, with his father long-since dead and his mother elderly and not moving around much any more, Greg had seemingly made some amends and gotten past the resentment he had.

He was doing the best he could now, having worked many odd jobs over the years, including selling Bibles, working at the Madison car wash, and doing some telemarketing for a collection agency. At least that's what his resume read. Edmund had not waited even 10 seconds after rehashing the old days to give Greg an impromptu interview in the human resources office as the generalists looked on, interrupted and stunned. Even 30-plus years later, an old-time athlete was able to utilize some measure of fame to get a foot in the door. It made Greg feel good to be recognized for something. He had been torched in the local press and especially in Helena for his inability to stop that touchdown pass. There had been a lot of hype about how great he was and was to become at the next level and the next level after that. The press can be cruel, and Greg could testify to that. Along with his tough home life, the press coverage made it even worse for him. Now someone who didn't even attend his high school was giving him a chance, treating him like the Madison cheerleaders did before that final game. He loved it.

Through his telemarketing gig in the 1980s, Greg learned how to talk his way into and out of things. So he wowed Edmund with talk of how much he admired Apache Foods and the contributions it had made to the region. Truthfully, Greg knew that he was reciting the About Us section of the Apache website; he had a feeling that Edmund wouldn't catch that. Greg was right. Regardless, positive words about a company in an interview can do nothing but help, especially if one is speaking to the most important person at the company when saying it. Edmund was hooked and told Greg that he would love to hire him right there on the spot.

Greg had come to Apache at a great time, especially considering that he was in his 50s now. Not many people in his age bracket got a fresh start at a new company. Apache was expanding its workforce to meet demand in its sweets line. Obesity was beginning to become a big problem in the United States, but like most companies, Apache knew that there were two kinds of people in the world: the kind who gorge and become obese; and the kind who eat a moderate amount of sweets and still have the discipline – or metabolism – to not overdo it. Either way, both consumer types were well taken care of with Apache's line of chocolate and lemon cupcakes, crème-filled snack cakes, and cookies, as well as the newer line of filled pies. While Greg had primarily worked office or light sales jobs, he expressed to Edmund that he would like a role that would allow him to "get his hands dirty" and concentrate on the task at hand. Greg expressed an enthusiastic interest in helping Apache continue its surge toward the top of the sweets market. Edmund could see that, and he had a perfect position for him.

A new line of candy was to be tested in several large metropolitan markets. Chocolate bars, peanut butter cups, and malted milk balls, popular for decades, were not included in Apache's lineup of offerings in the '70s and '80s, but the company risked falling behind if it didn't get involved. Daniel had been traveling for several weeks to find test stores and found some takers. He would be searching for a couple more months. The candy was a chocolate bar with very small bits of peanut, wafer, and lots of other things too, including coconut, pretzel, cookie, and nougat. It was a hybrid of several of the most popular candy bars in America, and a select group of employees loved the taste, so it was named the Everything Bar. Edmund told Greg that Apache needed a trustworthy and focused individual to oversee the assembly line for the new product, but he didn't mention where the test bars would be sent. That was confidential information, even to the employees. With all of the ingredients involved, there needed to be extra care taken to ensure that it was all done correctly in these initial test shipments. Daniel, always cognizant of his Indian roots, would normally test all of his new confections with the Indians on the reservations. In fact, there was a mission statement in the company handbook that included a reference to the Indian testing. But the Everything Bar needed a wider test audience. If people in the big cities liked this new candy bar, Apache could move to a new level of sales and notoriety that would end up helping the region and state even more than it already had. With no plans to expand locations and everything still done at the lone Rossage plant, the majority of the additional revenue would go directly to the local and regional economy.

Despite Greg's inner struggles, all that people outside of his home knew about him was that he was a great athlete, he became even more well known for his goat status in the big game, and he slipped into obscurity and became just another face in the Madison crowd. Having had all of those different jobs, though, endeared Greg to many types of people in the region, and his references would check out with flying colors. In fact, Edmund had the generalists check his references on the spot. A week later, Greg Farber began his new career as quality control technician for the new candy line of Apache Foods. Edmund was so proud of his new hire that he completely forgot to tell Daniel, although as co-owner, he wasn't obligated to mention it anyway.

Chapter 5

Edmund Chandler was always the trusting type. He never knew his mother, Mary, who died giving birth to him. He was raised by Howard during a time when all of the hardware store customers were friends or potential friends. Edmund knew the ins and outs of tools and small machinery by the time he was nine years old. And nobody in the town had a bad thing to say about him.

The similarities between him and Daniel were startling. Except for the fact that Daniel was an Indian and an athlete, the two were virtually the same person: smart, attentive, and caring, with father figures who were actually their fathers. They were college educated, and when Daniel visited the hardware store to ask about getting help starting the business, it was a match made in heaven. Daniel was a bit more outgoing, so he took it upon himself to make visits to store managers throughout Montana and the surrounding states to sell the products. Meanwhile, Edmund would get to be the mathematician and thinker. He would be in the office at least 10 hours each day, crunching numbers, fielding calls from Daniel if he was on the road, and doing all the office legwork. He trusted everyone with everything except the numbers. They were a good team, and things couldn't have been running more smoothly than they were on August 12, 1977.

On that day, Edmund walked toward the exit on the south end of the modest building Apache had built after a very successful year of operations. Edmund was reading some accounting paperwork and walking fairly briskly around a corner hallway when he smashed, face to face, into Tony, the mailman. Edmund's nose was bloodied and he fell, but it was seemingly a harmless encounter beyond that, something that happens probably hundreds of thousands of times a year in an office setting. But in this case, the expected headache Edmund had for the rest of that day continued into the next day, and the next week, and then the next month. Daniel, after weeks of watching Edmund suffer, could no longer contain himself and forced Edmund to see a doctor. Edmund had been "old school," and his father never saw a doctor, so why should he? A few weeks after blood tests were taken, the reasons he should have seen a doctor were explained to him. Edmund was told that when he ran into Tony, the episode triggered the rupture of a tumor lying dormant in the base of his skull. The tumor wasn't life threatening, but it would need to be removed and then Edmund's life would need to change drastically. He would be required to greatly reduce the stress in his life by taking a much smaller role in his company.

Edmund was devastated. A hardworking man, he and Daniel had built the company from the ground up and he desperately wanted to see the job through. They were only a few years into it, so the advice was a huge downer. But being the trusting man he was, Edmund heeded the doctor's words and sadly told Daniel that he would have to step down from his position as co-owner and CFO of Apache Foods. Daniel, however, would not hear of it. So after a few hours of back and forth in a small boardroom, the decision was made that Edmund would be Daniel's personal assistant in title and duties but that the pair would still share the profits equally. So Edmund's last official action as CFO was to hire Greg Farber. From then on, he gave some tips to Daniel but allowed other businessmen who came aboard as the company grew to wield more influence on day-to-day company decisions. It would stay that way for all the time Daniel and Edmund would be together, and it would save Edmund's life from becoming too stressful and from possibly ending altogether decades before it should.

Chapter 6

Greg Farber loved what he was doing. He was responsible for overseeing 10 people who worked solely on making the Everything Bar. The employees liked Greg from the start, which is not always the case when a new person comes in with no experience but all the authority to make decisions. But Greg was affable, and his reputation as a star athlete preceded him. Greg would make sure all of the employees followed their procedures to the letter, wearing the right equipment, sterilizing the machines, and having the ingredients in the right order for processing. Then he would stand with his clipboard and make sure that each bar was made in less than one minute. In short, Greg did his job correctly if each Everything Bar was nearly identical and had the same texture when someone bit into it. He was such a well-liked supervisor that within two months, he was named Apache Foods Employee of the Month by Edmund. Greg would show his appreciation for this accolade in a way that nobody could have ever foreseen.

Chapter 7

It was 80 degrees and balmy on an autumn day in South Padre Island, Texas. As Employee of the Month, Greg had been offered a trip for two to anywhere in North America. His colleagues were stunned that Greg had chosen this destination, but he wanted to go to South Padre Island, and to South Padre Island he went. The company ended up buying a ticket for one, as Greg decided to go by himself. Like Daniel and Edmund, Greg was single, never having settled into the married life like most of the small-town folks he grew up with. His relationships weren't easy and were, in fact, rare. Women were afraid of him becoming like his father, who was well known by the townsfolk as a powder keg and bar brawler. Even being a famous high school athlete couldn't save him from his father's bad acts. So Greg remained alone and childless throughout his life, with an occasional affair to pass the time and to remind himself that he was human. He had always wanted to venture out beyond Montana to find out what else was out there, and he had remembered seeing on television back in the '80s news clips of drunken teens partying through the day and night at South Padre Island. So he told his colleagues that he wanted to see where all the action had taken place.

Greg stayed at a modest hotel about eight blocks from the beach and had a routine during the five days he was there. Each morning he would wake up to the sounds of sea gulls, partake of the free Continental breakfast, and then venture down to the beach to stroll and let the water hit his feet for a few hours. He would then come back for lunch at the diner adjacent to the hotel, relax in his room, and then in the evening take a cab to the busy area of the island for happy hour and to take in the nightlife. It was a good time and a much-needed break from his routine at Apache and a diversion from remembering how tough he'd had it. But once Greg began to drink, a side of him was released that nobody, not even his father years ago, could have imagined.

On his third night in town, Greg went to a bar called The Straw Hut for happy hour. He had met a pretty lady there on his first night on the island and they got along well. On this night, though, there was nobody pretty sitting at the bar and a storm was rolling in. Greg, using the charm that got him the job at Apache, coaxed a bottle of whiskey from the young, vulnerable bartender, Maureen, in exchange for a gift. Greg had called the bar from Montana a week prior to ask what kind of crowd hung out there, and he had the good fortune of speaking with Maureen at the time. When he had asked her what kind of crowd to expect, she had said, "It's pretty eclectic, I'd say, but it ain't like my man Ethan Hawke's gonna show up." Apparently, this response churned the wheels of Greg's brain, and he had concocted a scheme to get a free bottle of liquor from Maureen. It worked. He produced a ruffled piece of paper with scribbled writing on it that he swore was Ethan Hawke's autograph that he had gotten at a comic book convention in Kansas City. Of course, none of this was true, but he figured that the crazier the story, in this party environment, the more likely she would be to believe it, and he was right. He had enough money for a bottle of any whiskey from a liquor store, but he reveled in getting it this way. Taking the full bottle back to his room, the rain began to come down in buckets almost as soon as he closed the door behind him. He opened the windows, turned on the television, and started drinking.

A drunken Greg Farber is an angry Greg Farber. After polishing off nearly all of the booze in a little more than an hour, Greg hurriedly and awkwardly stumbled to the hotel room door and left, courageously venturing out into a torrential downpour past the gazing desk clerk. He stopped at the diner and got a black plastic bag from the cashier. He stuffed it in his pocket and then staggered out and walked the eight blocks to the beach, which was, of course, abandoned. It was pitch black, but there was enough moonlight through the clouds and rain to see for several feet in front of him. It was hauntingly beautiful, yet somewhat frightening to see the waters of the Gulf of Mexico forever in the distance, dark and imposing. Greg finally got tired and sat down on a lonely log near an embankment and stared out into the gulf, cursing at the imaginary people he pointed to from his temporary stoop. He eventually passed out. Waking up a few hours later, he noticed that the rain had stopped and it was nearly dawn. The silence was deafening. Not even the water made much of a sound. Still, he was incensed for no apparent reason. He rose with a purpose from the log and strolled to the edge of the shore and looked down and around until he found what he was seeking. Ever so carefully, he picked up two jellyfish, put them in the black plastic bag, and stumbled back to the hotel. It was only Thursday, and he had another day left in town. But Greg packed his things, checked out of the hotel, and went back home to Montana a day early. He got home, and he put the plastic bag in his freezer.

Greg was a very intelligent and vengeful man. After the botched defensive play in high school, he would lock himself in his room and read his set of World Book encyclopedias his parents had gotten him when he was a young boy. He read nearly every word of every book, and he had discovered that the Irukandji jellyfish, native to the coast of Australia, was the most venomous jellyfish in the species. So when he noticed in 1998 that it had been spotted on South Padre Island just last year and had completely eradicated and replaced the inferior jellyfish that were present, he knew that all of the pieces could be in place. It took until September 16, 1999, for it to come together; but Greg could finally execute his plan.

Chapter 8

Daniel Smith took the day off for the first time in 20 years on Friday, September 17, 1999. He had just returned from the East Coast to secure stores to test the Everything Bar. He needed a break. With Edmund by his side, Apache Foods was now a state behemoth and he was worth at least $15 million.

Daniel had built a modest but luxurious home overlooking Lake Tanaka near Rossage a few years ago and lived there with Anna. He never did marry, although he dated long ago a woman from Helena for a couple of years before the relationship fizzled. He was pretty much a loner, but he didn't seem unhappy at all with that status. Edmund, on the other hand, appeared to be bothered, at times, that he had not found lasting love. Daniel was willing to live with whatever fate had in store for him, and as long as he had given his best effort, he could live with the results. Finally able to relax after a long and successful career to this point, Daniel sat down in his favorite recliner next to the fireplace. He didn't watch a lot of television but he was an avid reader and had primarily national newspapers, business periodicals, and sports magazines next to him in a small publication holder. Anna lived on the other side of the home and kept to herself. She was spry, though, so she walked around and got herself what she needed most of the time, stopping in to chat with her son for a few minutes each day and allowing Edmund to take her for a drive every now and then.

On this day, Anna was busy in her room, and Daniel was completely alone. He thought to himself that he would make it a point to go see Greg as soon as he could on the assembly line. It would be a great opportunity to shake hands with the man with whom he shared that infamous sports moment years ago. Wearing a smile on his face, Daniel leaned back in the recliner and drifted to sleep.

Chapter 9

Greg lived in the same Madison house his parents raised him in. After Hank died, he and Jean lived a quiet life. Memorabilia from his high school football days remained in the glass cabinet in the living room and he hardly noticed it when he walked through the room to the kitchen each day. Greg's own room, however, had been transformed into, all at once, a game room, chemistry lab, library, and drug den.

Nobody knew that Greg had been a habitual drug user for several years. His stash in the dresser drawer revealed a cornucopia of substances, including cocaine, marijuana, ecstasy, and other assorted pills. It's likely that he got them in Helena, which for Montana is the equivalent of Chicago for Illinois. Greg had been able to afford these drugs by staying employed, even though it cost him nearly all of his paychecks and plenty of the $60,000 in life insurance money left to him and Jean upon Hank's death. In the library area of the room sat a large desk with a computer and printer on it. The World Book encyclopedias were above the desk on a makeshift shelf. There were no other books in the room. And in the game room area was a color television and cable box, a video game system, and a stereo. All of the electronics were to the right of a bunk bed. Greg, like Daniel and Edmund, was an only child. But he alternated sleeping on the top and bottom bunks, even to this day.

Greg was pretty famous back in the day. On game days, he was a rock star at Madison High and was the best defensive player the state had seen in decades. Fast, handsome, and smart, Greg was a Montana girl's dream and the envy of many a man around the state. He wasn't even the quarterback, but his girlfriend was the head cheerleader. She dumped him a week after that last game, but that didn't stop Greg from still being popular around town. During the winter after football season ended, when most still thought he could recover somehow from the devastating knee injury, Greg went to Bozeman and got a chance to meet the president of the United States on his trip through the city in 1968. The president spoke at the science building at the University of Montana, where he was to congratulate a professor nominated for the Nobel Prize. So impressed was the president with Greg (he had asked a couple of questions during the press conference and wasn't even a reporter) that he jokingly recommended the school let him study to be a scientist. The president didn't know, of course, that the university had already rescinded the football scholarship they had offered him.

Greg, however, parlayed his successful conversation to gain an advance on Julie Adams, whose father, Dr. Fred Adams, was head of the science department and the Nobel nominee the president had come to see. Greg knew that Dr. Adams was responsible for the early development of stem cells at the school and, plotting his future actions years later, talked Julie into going out with him.

Julie and Greg had a scintillating affair that lasted all of three weeks, which was all the time Greg needed to seduce her into not paying full attention to him.

When she was asleep late one night, Greg grabbed her keychain and stole the key to the lab Dr. Adams gave his daughter in case something happened to him at work. Greg kissed Julie on the forehead and rode to the science building discreetly on a stolen bicycle left in the front yard of Julie's neighbor. He quickly used a side entrance at the science building and went up to Dr. Adams' lab, searching for two hours for what he needed. He found it labeled in the back of a freezer. Greg put two preserved stem cells of a human embryo that were in a liquid nitrogen solution into a sturdy container attached to his belt, and left. The next day, he put the key back on Julie's keychain while she showered. Greg then drove back to Madison, called Julie, and broke up with her. For 31 years, the cells had remained in his freezer.

Greg got home a day early from South Padre Island and walked into his room and shut and locked the door behind him. Some old, yellowish, and crinkled papers lay to the left of the computer. The top sheet read 'MIXTURE' and the third sheet under it read 'DIREC' before it was cut off by the sheet above it. He knelt next to the bed and began to pray, and he asked for assistance and the strength to carry out his actions and looked up at the ceiling, whispering "I am ready." He then went over and picked up the computer and printer, moving them to a smaller table nearby. He placed the black plastic bag he had on the now-cleared desk along with a set of test tubes, a Petri dish with a makeshift cover, two syringes, and some other items you would normally find in a chemistry lab. He donned the uniform and mask he was given by Apache and sat down to read the piece of paper titled 'MIXTURE.'

Greg used the syringe and drew one full amount of the extremely toxic and venomous fluid from the Irukandji jellyfish in the black plastic bag. In the Petri dish, he combined the substance with trace amounts of cocaine and heroin, and then added the stem cell solution and the final ingredient, a dead housefly. He took this solution with him to his car and started driving.

It was a sunny day in Madison, and Greg was content. He drove on the interstate without stopping or even turning his head for 30 minutes, suddenly veering off the road and onto a dirt pathway that he must have known was there beforehand. There would be almost no way to know about it otherwise. He drove another 15 minutes among the thick tree-lined dirt road and came upon an open area. It was a small Indian community far away from the reservations that were well known near Madison and Rossage. Greg stopped and turned off the car. He carefully carried his solution into one of several teepees, where an old Indian man wearing a brown shawl sat, intently looking at him as if to say that he was expecting him but still wasn't happy about it. Several other members of his tribe sat around him, all staring at Greg with disdain, despite knowing why he was there. Greg humbly told the old man, named Great Bear, that years ago he was the teenager who had come to him for help in creating a potion that would right a wrong. He had heard about the myth of Great Bear through a high school friend who was too afraid to investigate. But Greg wasn't scared of anything other than his dad; so here Greg was, all these years later. Great Bear remembered him from that day in 1968. He even said that he knew Greg would come back, no matter how long it took.

However, from the look on the faces of everyone in the teepee, there was a feeling that Greg wasn't intending to use the potion for good, and there was trepidation. But Greg, always the charmer, turned it on then. He said that he had waited for years and years to find the right situation with which to use the concoction and had finally done so and needed the final 'blessing' for it. He didn't have to elaborate, because Great Bear didn't ask him to. The other tribal members gave an odd look to Great Bear when he didn't ask any questions of Greg about exactly what the potion would be used for. But they were in no position whatsoever to question him about it. Great Bear asked him how he had ever found him to begin with, and Greg stated that back in '68, a local news reporter had written a story about the 'lost jungle Indian tribe' and that they represented an evil strain, as opposed to the docile and kind Indians who were already in the town (and able to be watched). Greg added that he so disagreed with the story premise that he wanted to find the tribe on his own and disprove the myth by using the services of the tribe himself. Of course, this was an enormous lie. His father hated Indians so much he would have easily killed one if given the opportunity, and because of his abuse of the family, Greg, not wanting to completely blame his father (or his mother for her inactivity), held the Indians responsible, as well. He hated them all. But he loved them right now. Nobody else back in '68 was remotely courageous enough to discuss the topic or dare to go into those backwoods (which had no dirt road then) to find the tribe to begin with. Great Bear sat silently for a few minutes, heaved and sighed quite loudly, and, without proof that he wouldn't use it for bad purposes, reluctantly began the blessing process by spitting his saliva into the solution. All five of the other tribal members present did the same. A pipe was lit and everyone partook of it, including Greg. After some chanting that Greg was silent for, the potion, still in the Petri dish, was handed to Greg and nobody said a word. Greg slowly got up and began to leave. As he exited, though, Great Bear made one final and important statement.

"If you do not use this potion for good, then you will surely die within two days. The gods will know immediately your intentions. Do not be foolish enough to test this prophecy. If you use this potion for bad intentions, then the person who swallows it will be permanently affected by it and have a lifetime of anguish. There is no antidote other than death. The potion will go into effect once the person who swallows it says the secret chant that only certain Apache Indians know. They are required to know the chant as a rite of passage, but it will never work unless they are the ones affected by the potion. One will know when he is affected by the potion. Destroy the directions you were given by me years ago to make this potion. I implore you once more to use it for the good of your fellow Indian friends. Now go. And do not ever return here, white man."

Greg drove back to his house with the solution sitting on the passenger seat next to him, and when he got back, he transferred it into the remaining unused syringe. It was 9 p.m. Greg went to sleep. He had a long Friday ahead of him.

Chapter 10

Greg woke up at 4:30 a.m. the next day, two hours before normal. He supervised the 9-to-5 shift but arrived, filled syringe in assembly line coat pocket, at 5:45 a.m. Nobody was there yet. He said hello to Al, the night watchman, and went to the main assembly room. Just yesterday, Edmund had informed Greg that the pretzel element of the Everything Bar would be removed because it was too salty and bread-like and didn't fit well with the other elements. Each ingredient had its own large tubular mechanism that drew a certain amount for each bar and 'plopped' it into its proper place on the conveyor belt. Greg was in charge of the machines, and this development was surprisingly great news for him. He left a note for Edmund stating that in order for them to remove the pretzel ingredient efficiently they should let one more batch go through with the pretzel to clear out the system entirely, since there was only one day's worth of pretzel left in the machine anyway. He then walked back to the machine after leaving the note, and emptied the syringe into the black rubber hose attached to the pretzel mechanism. The solution was extremely concentrated, and once inserted into the machine, it would not spread, as Greg thought. In fact, the potion would react in the opposite fashion, reducing in overall size and ending up in probably no more than one candy bar, and likely half of that one. Greg didn't know that. That day, business ran as usual and Edmund had no problem with letting the final candy batch proceed with the pretzel bits. Greg, thinking he had sentenced at least 10 hated Indians to a lifetime of hell on Earth, checked out at 5 p.m., said his usual goodbyes to the staff, and went home.

Greg had a good meal that night. Jean struggled to cook something for them and had left him some meat loaf. Greg made a sandwich along with some string beans and rice. Then he had some apple pie and washed it down with some iced tea. He went to his room, changed into some shorts and a t-shirt with the big lips from the Rolling Stones on it, and reached into the dresser drawer and smoked the last bit of marijuana he had left and walked down the hallway to kiss Jean goodnight. He never noticed that his mother had died. Jean lay on the bed as always, and he just assumed she was sleeping. Greg went back to his room and burned the old potion notes he had with a cigarette lighter, stamping them out gently as they turned to ashes on the floor. He gathered the materials he had used, the syringes, the Petri dish, the bag with two jellyfish, and the test tubes, and wrapped them in his Apache Foods lab coat, put the coat in a large shoe box – probably one for a pair of boots - and placed it in the bottom of his closet in the corner, right underneath his high school football letter jacket, hanging in the same place it had for 32 years. He turned the television off, sat on the edge of the bottom bunk of his bed, and methodically screwed a silencer to the end of the .38 he had taken long ago from his dad's closet. He stretched out on the bed, put the gun in his mouth, and pulled the trigger. Greg Farber was dead at 6:41 p.m. on Friday, September 17, 1999; and he had no idea that the Everything Bar he tainted would be tested on the East Coast long before it ever got to an Indian reservation in Rossage.

Chapter 11

Zack Williams is testy today.

"What the hell is wrong with where I'm standing? I'm not in anybody's way," he snapped to the airline representative taking boarding passes at the airport in Dallas. The rep had just politely asked Zack to move over a bit until his group number was called. But Zack saw through what he thought was fake Southern hospitality, and he was one to let people know in his own special way. Zack had a lot of his own special ways of thinking and doing things, and today was as good a day as any to showcase it.

Once on the plane and in his window seat, 7A, Zack leaned his head against the 'super-plastic pane,' as he called it, and stared at the grounds crew. They were hamming it up and telling jokes. Zack wondered if they had already planted a bomb on the plane and were playing it off to avoid suspicion. All he could do was pray, so he said a short one to himself: "Lord, please don't let this plane explode. My parents wouldn't be too happy about it. And they have spent too much money on me over the years to have me die before they do. Thanks buddy."

Zack Williams is an oddly interesting character study. He is 33 years old and sells advertising for The Executive Publisher, a New York-based firm specializing in gathering information about newspapers for potential advertisers to use in their decision-making process. Zack was a writer in a past life in Texas, but as much as he loved allowing his creative genius to flow through his fingers on the keyboard, it couldn't last. When he would turn in his tax forms stating that he had a gross annual income of $15,500, he knew he had to get out. Being patient and waiting intently for a big break in the writing business wasn't his game.

Born in New York City to black parents, Dorothy and Robert, who met at Princeton, Zack was an only child. He grew up until the age of 12 scouring the streets of Manhattan with his parents. Every several months back in the '70s, he would sneak out with his older cousins and spray paint subway trains. It was a miracle that he had never been caught.

When the family decided to pack up and leave for the greener pastures of Dallas in 1978, it didn't make a bit of difference to Zack. Grandma Lucille and Papa Carl lived there, and Cousin Benny was going to have a new and permanent playmate, whether he wanted one or not. Zack had grown up quite the shy one, afraid to express himself and fearful that if he did, someone would laugh at him and insult him. His parents, who were college professors, forced him into a very integrated kindergarten program in Harlem back in the late '60s so that he would be able to communicate with anybody from any background. The experiment had worked all these years later, as

Zack had a very eclectic and varied set of friends. But he also learned how cruel people could be toward one another at a young age, and it made him angry. There were lots of things that made Zack resentful when he was younger. Zack's other grandmother, Grandma Helen, was the valedictorian in her high school and college classes, but could not remotely get a job that matched her education upon graduation. This and other instances of what he considered disrespect made Zack mad.

Texas was a different animal for Zack. He went to Catholic high school but found that many of the students didn't quite practice what was preached to them. Like when he discovered two sophomores screwing in the chapel, or when his classmate called the study hall nun a whore and threw his math book at her. He lived in the area of Dallas called Oak Cliff. He learned over his high school years that white people in other parts of Dallas detested Oak Cliff for no other reason than there were a lot of blacks and Mexicans there. Not all of the blacks and Mexicans were quality people, though. Zack found that out when another black kid stole his bike at school and threatened to kill him when Zack tried to get it back. He returned it only when Robert came to the school and demanded the bike. Zack was made fun of at school for the episode, and the embarrassment and anger he felt stayed with him. Everything was bigger in Texas, according to the townsfolk and City Hall. But as Zack remembered, the only things bigger were a few shopping malls, the horizon, and pit barbecue sandwiches. Just about everything else was markedly smaller than where he was from. Zack loved being out in the sun as a teenager (although Dorothy didn't like it; she thought his complexion should stay the way it was when he was born: brown) and took every opportunity he could in summertime to play basketball at the local elementary school, which would open its doors for the kids to play every weekday all summer long. When he wasn't at the school, Zack was at Cousin Benny's place playing marathon games of Risk and Monopoly. So when his mother thought he was wasting his summers away, Zack was actually learning how to strategize, how to make deals, and how to think someone under the table. Who needs a novel for that, Zack would ask himself throughout high school.

Dorothy wanted Zack to be the next great black television host, but Zack didn't want to be on television, he wanted to be on the radio. Regardless, Zack always agreed with his mother, smiled, and kept on walking. Zack thought Dorothy had maple syrup instead of blood, because she was that sweet a person. Zack never forgot her stories about having to pick up her food sometimes in the back of the restaurant or drink from the colored water fountains growing up. He couldn't imagine having to do that himself, and he tried to put it out of his mind because it would anger him even more.

Robert was the opposite of Dorothy. He could have cared less if Zack was on television or not. As long as Zack made it to the age of 30 without being shot to death, particularly by another black man, Robert felt his accomplishments were golden. But both parents were extremely intelligent, down-to-earth, and real people. They placed a premium on learning and said early on to Zack that independence and thought led to creativity and purpose. "But if you ain't got no degree, you won't be independent for too long," Dorothy would sometimes say with a hint of slang and a head tilt. And she was right. His parents were somehow always right.

Zack became a cynical, emotional, engaging, witty, graphic, angry, charming, and deceptive adult, pretty much the opposite of his childhood, except for the emotional part. Part of him was incredibly resentful at what his family and the families of people he didn't even know had gone through just so that he could vote or hang out at the bar or go to school. He used his anger at times as a badge of honor. He felt that he had the right to be angry, and if anyone asked him why, he was always prepared to tell anyone who would listen all about his experience and that of the family and friends he knew. But he rarely looked angry. He just *was* angry. He made friends easily across all boundaries and social strata. His parents shaped and made what was good about Zack, but he molded a bit of goodness and most of what was bad about him from a combination of factors, including the people he knew and came across, things he read and watched, movies, songs, pornography, and the streets. Zack had been around a bit, and he had been to some places nobody knew he had been or thought he would ever go. But despite his bitterness and rising level of frustration, he garnered respect and admiration, and most of Zack's friends loved his folks and treated them like a second set of parents. It made Zack realize that so many of his friends had parents they either didn't like or didn't know how to communicate with. And he felt fortunate and thankful as he peered out of the plane window in seat 7A waiting to back out of the gate. The older he got, the more he hated leaving his parents behind so far away in Texas. But he had no choice on this September Friday.

"We'd like to welcome you to Flight 768, with nonstop service to New York City," the flight attendant said. Zack wasn't too politically correct and thought to himself, "Why doesn't anyone call them airline hostesses any more?" Once the flight got airborne, Zack began his ritual to pass the time: as much reading of sports magazines as possible followed by humming the album or a set of songs of his choice to the exact note that it would be had he been listening to them on a set of headphones. Zack was strange that way. He preferred challenging himself to hum the tunes, singing the lyrics in his head if need be, rather than simply listening to the songs he wanted to on a portable device. Strange indeed. But it was *his* strange and nobody else's. So after he finished reading, he started humming the first song to himself. He then kept right on going all the way through 20 of his favorite tunes, before he drifted off for a nap. An hour later, he had landed safely in Queens. It was time to be a New Yorker again.

Chapter 12

"What's up nigga?? Where you been?" asked Puerto Rico Ron, not even five seconds after Zack walked into Maurice's, on 74th St. on the upper east side of Manhattan. Zack had taken a cab from the airport, dropped off his bags at his first-floor apartment in Queens, and taken the subway directly to the bar.

"I'm chillin' man, what's going on, big Ron?"

Their legendary handshake was a simple clasp of the palms, but the impact of the two hands together was so forceful that it often made the bar vibrate to people within a foot or two of them. "Get me a box. I see you saved me a seat. You're a gentleman, but I don't know about a scholar."

The box was what the locals commonly referred to when speaking of the bar's trivia game, a national trivia contest that was played on the bar televisions. Maurice's would compete with bars around the nation who were hooked into the same network. But most importantly, the patrons at the bar competed against each other; and alcohol was the great equalizer. Zack and Ron threw back a couple of inaugural whiskey shots to get things rolling. "Ahhh, the sweet nectar of the gods," Zack often said after downing a whiskey and slamming the shot glass on the bar. As the two began their game, they discussed, as always, how things were going in the big city, general small talk. But Ron was anything but small.

A large man, Puerto Rico Ron had a gray beard and sideburns and resembled Fidel Castro. He was probably in his mid-to-late 50s, a Marine long ago who had cultivated a teaching career in NYC public schools into a soon-to-be early retirement. But nobody knew when that would be. Ron was notorious for never revealing two things: his age or his true thoughts. But he and Zack had a connection. They understood each other and often discussed imbalances in society once the 'nectar of the gods' drowned them out.

"White people, Zack, fuckin' white people. They're something else," Ron said. "Yo los puedo mascar pero yo no los puedo tragar!" Zack needed a translation. Ron said it meant that he could chew them, but he could not swallow them. This statement stayed with Zack for some time.

Zack had seen a lot of racism in his day, most of it directed at him. Yet he also had met some fantastic white people in his life, through his parents' jobs, in high school, in college, at work. Unfortunately, the scales were tipped a bit more on the racist side. So over the years, he grew a bit more cynical and untrusting of whites, until they proved to him they could be trusted. It worked the other way around, too. Most whites, in Zack's experience, didn't trust anyone who was darker than they were. But the way Zack saw it, their lack of trust was based on feeling guilty for their own bad treatment of the same people they feared. So more often than not, he didn't care if whites trusted him or not. Because it was never going to be justified, in Zack's mind. Ron's statement was more indicative of an unavoidable reality that happens to minorities as they get older: the realization that they will never see in their lifetime an America where they won't be called a spic or a nigger, Zack thought. And that realization can be like a weight bench placed right in the middle of one's back.

Ron had told Zack once that he had his six children by three different women so that he could have as many kids as possible live different life experiences and try to extend his family through generation after generation, hoping that one of his relatives down the line actually lives in a different and better America. The more kids, the better the odds, he said. It was midnight, and Zack was tired from the flight. He bid Ron adieu, and took the long subway journey home to Queens. Laying on his cherry-wood futon in his one-room apartment, Zack looked up at the ceiling, wondering what tomorrow would bring. His eyes closed, and then he prayed that they would open again, so he could find out exactly what tomorrow had brought.

Chapter 13

The west side train in Manhattan took a painfully long time to get to Penn Station. Zack had a huge bag of Christmas gifts with him. It contained at least eight presents, some larger than others. But he wasn't headed to a hospital to give the gifts away to sick children. He was going up to Washington Heights to see Paulina and be her Santa Claus for the evening. And Zack hoped that she had more than some cookies and milk for Santa near the fireplace. He arrived at her apartment building off of Fort Washington Avenue and got a big kiss, a big smile, and a long hug. He had just gotten in that night from a trip to see the family for the holidays, so it had been a while.

Paulina was in a hurried mood and seemed tired and tense, probably from cooking, as Zack could smell something spicy coming from the kitchen. He had come at just the right time, a bit earlier than expected, and she looked like she could use one of his patented massages. She closed the door and he put down the big bag of items and told her that he needed to use the restroom because the train ride was so long. She said, "You know where it is babe, hurry back." As Zack walked down her long hallway to the restroom, he reflected quickly about how Paulina was a quiet, cerebral type with a good heart, an attractive teacher from Russia who would do anything for her students. They had been dating for six months. Zack got to the restroom and closed the door halfway. It was far from the front of the apartment, so no need to close it for a quick pee session. He walked over to the toilet. The seat was up. Zack's mouth got dry all of a sudden. The television came on up front. It wasn't on when he arrived. When he flushed the toilet, he heard a door close in the background of the noise the toilet made. Zack has never been a dumb man, and so he immediately thought to himself, "Paulina is a bitch. I can't believe it."

Once Zack has been let down, sometimes even if he thinks incorrectly that he has been let down, there is no turning back. He is extremely giving of himself and goes all out in his relationships. He could forgive, but he could not forget. He quickly zipped his pants, knowing he had been played. Walking briskly back to the front, he didn't stop to acknowledge Paulina, he simply opened her front door, seeing the outline of a large, muscular man in a bubble coat descending down the staircase far in the distance.

"You locked the door when I got here. It isn't locked now," Zack said calmly to Paulina. "A man is hurrying down the staircase of your building, the television you never watch is suddenly on, you're cooking Latin food you never cook, and your toilet seat is up. Why the fuck didn't you just tell me you were seeing someone else? I'm 33 years old! Kiss my ass. I'm outta here."

Before he left, Zack took one of the gifts, a pair of gold earrings that cost him $200, out of the huge bag and put it in his coat pocket. No way was she getting that gift, Zack thought, and he still had the receipt for it. Paulina sat stunned on the couch. She didn't even say anything. She was caught, and she knew it. Zack had gotten her a toaster oven because hers was old and worn out. He took that gift and threw it as hard as he could at her television, knocking it off its stand and breaking the screen, causing sparks to fly. Enough of the wrapping paper on the gift was torn so that Paulina could clearly see that it was a toaster oven. Realizing how she had made a big mistake, she began crying and apologizing, and she stood up and began to walk over. Zack hurriedly left and slammed the door behind him. Paulina didn't get to the door in time and her right pinkie finger got caught in the door, virtually exploding and being severed in the process. She screamed so loudly that two neighbors ran to their doors and opened them to see what the problem was. One immediately called 911. Zack descended down the same set of stairs the mystery man in the bubble coat had a few minutes earlier. Deep down, Zack wanted to meet up with the man for a drink and find out what he did to get Paulina to fuck him. But he thought better of that ridiculous notion and went to the subway station and home. He had caught a glimpse of the pool of blood and Paulina's finger swimming in it as he went down the steps. It was more than enough for him. He had just last week changed his phone number because it was too hard for people to remember, and it was unlisted. And Zack was one of the last bastions of people who didn't have a cell phone yet. He was going to get one next week. On top of that, Paulina had never come over to his place in Queens and never asked where he worked. She was selfish like that. So Paulina was shit out of luck trying to contact him, Zack thought, smiling.

Zack left his alarm on by mistake. It was 6:30 a.m. He made it to Saturday in a cold sweat. And, thankfully, he had never even met anyone named Paulina.

Chapter 14

Zack woke up and turned on the television. He watched a sports show each and every day of his life. Since the show repeated itself over and over early in the morning, he would watch the program once, and then leave it on, muted, and turn on the stereo. His musical choices were varied. Zack was an old-school type, so he enjoyed a mixture of the music he grew up with that his parents played and the music his parents didn't like that he heard on the radio back in the '70s and '80s. He had a compilation CD he bought that included old school R&B, bebop jazz, classic rock, and early hip hop. He played the CD, and climbed on the elliptical machine he had squeezed into his apartment. His stamina was down, and he could only do 20 minutes before stopping, climbing off, and staggering toward the bathroom for a shower.

He climbed slowly into the tub and turned the knobs. As the lukewarm water descended over him, Zack stood there, eyes closed, mouth open, thinking. Zack was a thinker. He was pleased with his professional life as a sales rep and ex-writer, but he wasn't pleased with his personal life. His ego was massive on the inside, but seemed like only an act on the outside. His friends never thought he was an egomaniac, just someone who sometimes acted like one as part of a joke or statement he needed to make. Zack was a very intelligent man, but he didn't care for showing that through his grades in school or by discussing what or how many books he had read. Books were boring to Zack. He didn't care what someone else's interpretation of love or the universe was. So when he read a book, it was nonfiction, something that had actually happened, tangible, touchable. The abstract was meaningless, because Zack couldn't see it. As a result, he didn't particularly like certain forms of entertainment, like science fiction films. He thought they were bullshit, because they weren't real and could never possibly happen. He was the only person he had ever known who hated *Star Wars* when it came out. He thought it was stupid. Actually, Zack thought he may have very well been the smartest man in the world and that he lived on another planet. He thought that most of the people he knew were simply beneath him in intellect. Zack would shape his conversations so that he wouldn't stray too far ahead mentally of the people he knew. He was incredibly impatient when someone didn't catch on to something that, to Zack, was painfully obvious or right there in front of him.

On one occasion, at a bar, someone who Zack had met said he didn't like sports and that it bored him and that he loved to read and had books upon books at his apartment. Zack hated him from that point forward. He didn't like people who weren't well rounded like he thought himself to be. The man didn't have to adore sports, all he had to do was like sports and also like books, and Zack would have been more open to him. But Zack grew up believing that all men needed sports in their lives to confirm that they had a competitive streak beyond the classroom or board game, and he simply did not understand the makeup of someone who didn't agree with that notion.

Zack was heterosexual and had several relationships. He was a liberal and he was sly, so it wasn't beneath him to befriend gay men in order to gain access to their attractive female friends. In fact, he would often leave the sly part out and tell his gay friends back in Texas that he was hanging out with them specifically for that reason. Thinking back, Zack determined he had met five of his lovers through gay men, and he had known seven gay men overall. An excellent ratio, he thought. He didn't know any gay men in New York, although he knew plenty of straight men who he thought might as well have been gay by the dumb decisions they made with women.

Over the last few years, Zack became lonely. He had approximately six lovers a year, which he thought was about average. Cousin Benny routinely would tell him that a story he read stated that the average man slept with seven women over the course of his lifetime. Zack would always say that the story was based on the sex lives of Eskimos and couldn't possibly be true. But the fact that he had a high amount of lovers over the years eventually led to Zack not feeling fulfilled in his soul. Of course, he eventually blamed his lack of having found the relationship of a lifetime on the stupidity of the women he met. They always did something to piss him off and break the trust bond he had developed with them. He may have said the wrong thing from time to time or forgot something important every blue moon, but he didn't cheat on any of his girlfriends, and he thought that was what was most important. Zack believed that if he was a good man, treated women with respect and kindness, was humble, polite and didn't stray from a woman he was dating, that he would be rewarded with the same behavior. But his last three girlfriends cheated on him. He found out in different ways, as none of them owned up to their actions. With all three of them, he was too afraid of being alone and never dumped them, getting dumped instead, which is probably why he immediately dumped Paulina in his dream. He couldn't do it in reality.

Zack was raised in the Methodist church, his mother Dorothy having been a church regular growing up in Texas. But Robert didn't care about church, so the regular family visits stopped, and eventually Dorothy went alone, occasionally bringing Zack along. Zack considered himself to be spiritual and to have an excellent relationship with God. He had a keen respect for other religions. He thought that there was probably one being that created everything and that different cultures called him by different names. Zack didn't even know if it was a 'him.' God could easily have been a female or some other form. Zack just communicated well with whatever God was. He either prayed or had a conversation nearly every night with God and felt that was enough to stay on the good side of the ledger. Zack was an athlete and a fairly handsome man with a light moustache and the occasional gruff beard. His voice was soothing and nontraditional. It wasn't too deep and it wasn't too high-pitched either. Every woman he ever encountered said his voice made them swoon or, at the very least, take notice and pay attention. He was 5-foot, 10-inches tall. His weight varied between 190 and 230 pounds, depending on his mood and how busy he was at work. He gained and lost weight quickly, a dangerous thing, said his doctors, when he took the time to go and see one.

Zack played one sport, basketball; he was a shooting guard, and he was good at it. On the basketball court, he was timid as a youth and let other players talk trash to him. One opponent in high school even jumped with him to try to block his shot, and when Zack released the ball, the opponent grabbed his fingers and tried to twist them off. Zack had a gulf of resentment toward everyone he played basketball against, because they always thought that his demeanor, his voice (which was called 'proper' in the South), and his shyness translated into him being weak and inferior. By the time he got to college, Zack had a lot of angst built up, and he let it out on the court. He played so fiercely and beautifully - once independent of his parents and out of high school - that he garnered a following. People would actually show up at the gym to watch Zack play against the scholarship players, and he would dominate them. He tried out for the university team, and he made it. But after two weeks of doing nothing but eating, sleeping, studying, and hanging out with the team, Zack knew that it wasn't for him. He missed his friends, and the binge drinking at frat parties, and the half-assed studying at the library, and the late-night runs to the hot dog stand. He quit the team, satisfied that he exorcised his demons and everyone knew he could compete. Naturally, over the years Zack allowed his ego and inner loneliness to make him bitter and cynical. And even though he had the capacity to be incredibly rude, judgmental, and straightforward, he was still considered a nice person who would reach out and help the next man if he truly needed it. And he called his parents every day.

Snapped out of his thinking session under the shower head by the phone ringing, Zack picked up the bar of soap, lathered the washcloth, and cleaned himself. The long shower over, Zack prepared for his typical Saturday afternoon ritual, which was meeting up with the crew for all-day drinking, sports watching, trivia playing, and male bonding at Maurice's. The crew consisted of Puerto Rico Ron, Al, George, Kent, Stevie, and Johnny. These were the guys Zack hung out with since moving back to New York in 1998. He didn't know that much about them, possibly because he didn't care to get too close, but he knew enough about each to be loyal to them all. The caller who phoned while Zack was in the shower was Ron. He left a message saying that plans had changed and the crew was now meeting at TapTown, another bar down the street that used to cater to a lot of New York baseball players when it was named something else several months ago. No big deal, Zack thought. So everyone met there, exchanged hugs, and waited for Al to buy the first round of beer and shots.

Al was a divorced Jewish accountant for a small but busy firm in Manhattan. He hated his ex but was thankful they had no children.

George was a tall black man who could have had a much more commanding presence if he wanted to. He was a private type who knew how to give just enough information about himself to shut everyone up and keep his secrets buried.

Kent was the West Indian doctor and the one with the most in common with Zack. He was from Queens also, and knew how to get women, mostly because he was the best looking of the group, made big money, and didn't really have to do all that much. The fact that he was also charming just increased the tally for him that he would have had simply by showing up.

Stevie was the one everybody else had to watch out for. He was short on common sense and long on cockblocking. Stevie had no idea when to hold or when to fold, Zack thought. When a married man asked Zack about Stevie once, Zack told him, "If you were a single man and Stevie was around, God help you; because either he will ruin it for both of you, or he will ruin it for both of you." Stevie wasn't the type of cockblocker who got the girl.

Johnny was the reserved and classic gentleman. Nobody got too loud with Johnny other than Ron, who didn't care who he got loud with. Johnny was the type to discuss the tab with the bartender or talk politics with the unrefined guy next to him on the sly while the rest of the group yelled and high-fived over a football play. The crew sat down at the bar and noticed its stylish wooden décor and clean taps. They were the only people at the bar. It was about 2 p.m. After a couple of shots of whiskey and the second round upon them, bought by George, someone walked in. Zack, whose face was staring at the bottom of a frosted mug of brew as he finished off his first cold pint, was the only one who didn't notice. But he did notice how suddenly quiet it had gotten.

"Who died fellas?" Zack asked with a smile. Stevie tilted his head back a bit and shifted his eyes at Zack and then quickly to his left to indicate that he should look that way. Walking toward the back of the bar and descending down a staircase was a woman in a white coat, jeans, and a red sweater. She was decent looking with a nice body, from what Zack could tell. But he wasn't really paying attention. He was into his drinking and male bonding, and he didn't really care about women today. So he started talking about football while everyone else's attention was elsewhere. Eventually, the others joined Zack and things were back to normal. Not 10 minutes later, the hush came over the guys again, and again Zack was in his element, lifting the frosty mug to his lips. This time, however, he joined the others in silence.

Zack was a cool customer. After years and years of dating, heartbreak, and having been with more than a hundred women, he knew the drill. But as he had heard others say for so long, this was different. The woman standing in front of him was about 5-foot, 7-inches tall. She asked if he wanted another beer, and Zack nodded approvingly with a look on his face of both confusion and pleasure. Zack didn't quite understand how someone could look like this. Kent introduced himself and extended an arm past Zack and toward the bartender. She smiled gently and said "Nice to meet you Kent, my name is Victoria."

Victoria was the most beautiful person Zack had ever seen. She was Puerto Rican, meaning she had African, European, and Indian roots. Each of these was represented perfectly, Zack thought immediately. She took care of the Indian part with her jet black and incredibly shiny and long hair that stopped just above her waist in the back. She was fair skinned and her eyes reminded Zack of the greenish-blue marbles he played with as a youth in Texas with Cousin Benny. That took care of the European part; and she had Africa covered. She had somewhat of a broader nose, lips thicker than molasses, and curves that only a German autobahn driver could truly appreciate.

As the crew fumbled among themselves to get a word in, Zack kept quiet and stared at Victoria like a child stares at a cartoon. She noticed but wasn't offended, probably because Zack's stare was more like an appreciative applause with the eyes, as opposed to the perverted glare. His egomaniacal thoughts of being intellectually superior to all of his acquaintances had kicked in, and he would coolly sit and wait for a moment alone to make his sales pitch. The moment came when Victoria, stressed out over something, asked the bar manager if she could go outside for a cigarette. She didn't know Zack could hear her request, and she was caught off guard when Zack was standing outside already when she arrived.

"Taking a break from all us daytime heathens, huh?"

"You heathens are sure better than the people I'm used to dealing with."

"Well, you're dealing with Zack Williams now," Zack said confidently, extending his hand. Smiling and clearly impressed by the witty response, Victoria returned the handshake, saying nothing but staring out into the overcast Manhattan sky, blowing a steady stream of smoke and exhaling with apparent relief.

"I'm Victoria, by the way, sorry about that pause. I am totally in left field today, and I don't even smoke." Zack thought to himself that Victoria could play left field, or any other position on his baseball team.

"No problem," he said. "From what I gather, the only people New York women really need to answer to immediately are their parents, their best friend, and their lover. Nobody else really matters. Is this true?"

"Isn't that true for all of us?"

"No," Zack said flatly.

"OK, I understand," she flatly countered. "Listen, I gotta get back behind the bar, but it was nice to meet you." She left him with the most fake smile he had ever seen, and Zack was floored. Left to ponder his error, Zack figured he would make up for it in front of the group because he had no choice. He knew Victoria would never go back out to smoke again.

Zack went back inside but passed the bar to use the restroom first. He went downstairs and around a corner, finally arriving at the large wooden door labeled 'MEN.' It seemed to Zack like he was entering an office building where he would get silent advice to use once he left. Standing at the urinal, he pondered his newest crush with as much calm as possible. He had no thoughts other than she was stunning and he wanted her. He went back up to the bar, sat in his seat, waited for Victoria to serve a few other people at the other end of the bar, and then gave the signal that he needed another drink. Victoria walked calmly down to his end, without a smile to be seen.

"You know who else matters, Victoria? God, your boss, and me," he said. "Those are three people who you also should always respond to immediately."
Giggling a bit and sensing the challenge inherent in the statement, Victoria dove in headfirst.

"And why should I immediately answer to someone I met 10 minutes ago at a bar?"

"Because you grew up with everyone answering to you. And just about the time you're ready to answer to someone, you end up giving that privilege to a good-looking asshole who didn't appreciate the opportunity, wasn't smart enough to realize that it didn't mean you do whatever he says all the time, and treated you like the trophy wife you may think you are. But you aren't."

Victoria walked away expressionless while the now-drunk crew patted Zack on the back and laughed at him.

"Nice try, Professor Williams," Stevie said.

"Drunk mufucka gettin' all philosophical and shit," was the reply from Kent. The others just laughed. Zack laughed along with them, of course, but this was not just an ordinary attempt to hit on a woman for him. This, as they say, was different.

Victoria left work a half hour later, and said goodbye to everyone with a smile, thanking them for their tips and service. Ron, a bartender loyalist, asked what her schedule was for future visits. She said Monday, Wednesday, Thursday, and Saturday, shooting an ever-so-quick glance at Zack as she spoke. Zack knew he would be back on Monday.

The guys left TapTown about a half hour after Victoria did and headed over to Maurice's to keep the party going. It was a particularly good time this Saturday night, and Zack attributed it to everyone subconsciously having had their day brightened by the appearance of the beautiful Victoria. As much as he knew that a woman like her had literally hundreds and hundreds of wanton suitors, Zack could not take his mind off of her. It was pure lust. After all, he didn't know her remotely well enough to consider any other feelings. And being the emotional but practical realist that he was, love at first sight simply didn't register with Zack; no such thing, he thought, it was all lust until a bona fide reason to feel differently arrived. He struggled with it all evening at Maurice's. He put up a brave front, shooting pool, continuing to get more and more inebriated, flirting, bonding, and seemingly having a great time relaxing. And he did have a good time, just not great like others might have thought. The image of Victoria from the side, arching her back to pour tap beer into a glass, was killing him, as he imagined it was probably killing hundreds of others at the very same time.

Zack didn't like competition very much, mostly because he thought, of course, that his competitors for women were usually stupid. If Zack saw a man talking to someone he was interested in who he genuinely thought was better than him, he was more than happy to step aside. Even if he thought the guy was inferior mentally, he wouldn't interfere. When Zack had relationships, he thought it was the woman's job, not his, to regulate the actions of other men. Chivalry was alive with Zack, but it had its limits. And if he thought that a woman was trying to make him a bit too jealous and overextending herself toward someone else, trust would evaporate, and so, too, would the relationship. Zack realized that his ways opened him up to criticism and accusations of paranoia and jealousy, but he didn't care. He had seen much worse from acquaintances and friends over the years, including several women who dated men he considered to be much more sexist and behavior-challenged than he might have been.

It was 3 a.m., time to go home after a night of fun with the guys. Zack bid farewell to his buddies and began the long subway trek to Queens.

Chapter 15

Daniel Smith was excited about the new candy bar line. The Everything Bar was tasty, and he and Edmund just knew it would be a big hit. They couldn't wait for the sales results from Baltimore, Philadelphia, and New York City, the three eastern cities in which Daniel was able to get a few convenience stores to allow him to sell it. The stores agreed to put up small displays right at the counter to entice customers to do an impulse grab at something new. Now it was time to continue improving the existing business and wait for the results of the new product.

After talking with Daniel about the developments, Edmund went back to his office, right next to Daniel's. He was pleased. It had been a week since the last batch of Everything Bars were produced and shipped out to the test markets. Greg had done an excellent job of overseeing the test batch and was taking his much-deserved week-long trip for being Employee of the Month. This was Friday, the last day of Greg's vacation, and Edmund was looking forward to discussing possible new concepts on Monday for Greg to go over with the assembly line staff. Edmund's phone rang. There was a long pause after an initial greeting. Edmund hung up, slowly got up from his desk and walked back over to Daniel's office. Daniel asked him what was wrong, as Edmund had a depressed look on his face.

Edmund said plainly, "Greg Farber is dead."

Chapter 16

Vilanova County Sheriff Chris David was a large man with a commanding presence, a rotund belly, and a no-nonsense attitude. He was closing in on middle age, but with that he also was gaining as much wisdom along the way. He was a 29-year veteran of the department and had closed dozens of felonies along the way, from armed robberies to the few murders that happen in a remote Montana county. The same praise David received couldn't be heaped upon most of the people who worked for him, however, including 22-year-old deputy Farley Thomas, who David thought was the closest thing to Barney Fife the sheriff's office had seen in the nearly 150-year history of Vilanova County. But he wasn't in charge of hiring; the state was, so he dealt with it as best he could.

"Hey Chief, take a look at this!"

Thomas had found something in Greg Farber's bedroom. David sauntered over, told him to step back a bit, and decided that this would be a good piece of evidence to collect. Thomas, in an attempt to look like he was in charge of the situation, called a subordinate detective in to put the evidence, a half-inch, slightly burnt piece of yellowish paper, in a baggie. David rolled his eyes, remembering how Thomas had tried to be funny earlier. When they first got to the scene, Thomas had said, "I guess this man ain't got no satisfaction for life no more," a clear reference to the Rolling Stones t-shirt Greg had worn as his final outfit. David didn't think it was funny at the time, and he hadn't changed his opinion now. Glancing over at Greg, laying on the bottom of the bunk bed with his eyes wide open and his blood and brains freshly covering the pillow under his head like a drunken college student's vomit, David stepped outside for a cigarette.

Greg, who still had part of the silencer resting on his mouth and a grip on the gun when discovered, had been found about two hours prior, after the next door neighbors, whose bedroom window is only three feet away from Greg's, smelled something foul. They hadn't seen anyone come in or go out of the home in over a week, but they hadn't called police before because, quite frankly, they didn't speak to the Farbers and didn't care that much about whether they were going in or out. Only the stench of death prompted the call on this Sunday afternoon. Jean was found where Greg had left her, laying dead on her bed, leaned on her side. County residents were shocked at the headlines on Monday: *Former Madison Grid Star Commits Suicide*. It was the talk of all the towns for miles around. But there would be much more to discuss in the coming months.

Chapter 17

Zack would have been motionless, were it not for the constant vibration and rocking motion of the Queens-bound train. He was drunk, but he knew the drill. Go out, meet the fellas, have a good time, get on the train, give "go fuck yourself" looks to sober and mightier-than-thou jackasses who give him strange looks, get home, watch television, and pass out. That was many a single man's routine in New York, so if it was fine for the others, it was fine for Zack. He figured that he would differentiate himself by being the smart talker and the one who knew how to talk to women. Even trashed on the subway at close to 4 a.m., Zack's ego raged to manic proportions.

Finally stopping at Kew Gardens, Zack climbed slowly up the stairs and shuffled to the bodega two blocks from his apartment. It was open all night, and thank God for that, Zack thought, because he needed something to eat. He didn't want to get anything too filling, because he had been craving pizza for over a month and was determined to have some while he watched football on Sunday, or in about eight hours, since it was already Sunday. So he grabbed a bottle of iced tea from the refrigerated soda section. His elbow knocked over a couple of plastic bottles of soda. Bending slowly to pick them up and return them, he looked up to the hateful gaze of Vendi, the Pakistani clerk who has had a running feud with Zack for months. Vendi thought Zack bought beer for a minor last year, and Zack told Vendi that the 16-year-old in question was his visiting nephew, who was just carrying the bag of beer for him on the way home. It was a lie, but it was all Zack could come up with at the time. The minor had actually given Zack 20 bucks to get him a six pack of beer and keep the change. Not a bad deal, so Zack took it.

"Where's your goddamn nephew tonight?" asked Vendi. He asked the question nearly every time Zack entered the bodega, which wasn't that often any more. "You lying motherfucker."

"I don't know how many times I gotta tell ya man, he was just carrying the bag," Zack slurred. "Just ring up my shit." Zack grabbed a candy bar at the counter and tossed it with the iced tea and paid the two dollars.

"When I find your nephew, I am gonna have both of you arrested,"Vendi said, obviously reaching for words now, nearly a year after the incident.

"Find my nephew? Motherfucker, you need to find your mind, you obviously lost it somewhere around here." Zack snatched the candy bar and iced tea bottle and left.

As always, Zack went into his apartment, put his keys and wallet in the catch-all on his dresser, took off all of his clothes, turned the television on to a cable station he had never watched, urinated, and laid on the futon. The movie was boring, whatever it was. He turned to the sports channel. A story was on about basketball, Zack's favorite sport. Paying attention, Zack sat up on the futon and grabbed the candy bar.

The package was bright red with brown and gold writing. He thought he had picked up something he had eaten before, but this was definitely not anything he'd seen. The bold writing spelled 'EVERYTHING' on the front of the package. "Oh well," Zack thought aloud, and he opened it and took a big, drunk man's bite. He chewed on it while he watched the hoops report, concentrating on both the television and his taste buds. His forehead got creases in it. That meant that he liked what he tasted. He laughed aloud as he said to no one in particular, "Damn, Everything is right! There's all kinds of shit in this bar!" But it was all kinds of good, with a bit of a twang to it toward the end, and he wolfed it down in a couple of minutes, washing it down with the iced tea in eight solid gulps. He put the candy wrapper inside the plastic iced tea bottle, threw it on the floor, leaned back, turned the TV off, and was out a minute later.

As it turned out, Saturday had brought with it the same old Saturday.

Chapter 18

Victoria Delgado got out of the cab in East Harlem Saturday evening from her shift at TapTown and walked up the four flights of stairs to her one-bedroom apartment. She placed her purse on the stainless steel countertop, walked calmly to the restroom, washed the makeup from her face, used the toilet, and looked at herself in the mirror to check her skin. Victoria had vitiligo, a skin condition that causes a loss of pigmentation and discoloring in certain areas. Only one percent of the population has this condition. A man Victoria met once at a nightclub said she was the most beautiful woman to ever have vitiligo. She wore hers like a badge of honor, which was easy for a woman of her beauty to do. The condition never caused her to lose the attention of men or the jealousy of women. Victoria didn't have many female friends, despite being a kind person and very witty. She was somewhat goofy and easily able to laugh at herself.

At a young age, she was a classically trained pianist and was one of the top ballet students in her class. In college in Florida, she was an economics whiz and enjoyed history, planning to one day work as an assistant district attorney in New York City. Her family owned a group of clothing stores in the five boroughs called Delgado's. The stores were so successful that Victoria and her sister, Emily, were debutantes who mastered the art of being classy in public. Victoria attended a prestigious all-girls school before college and was called upon numerous times for modeling gigs starting at age 17, from classic wedding dress shoots to hot bikini sessions for low rider magazines. A modeling website she belonged to stated that she was 28 years old and that her measurements were 36DD-25-37.

Victoria had a wild side. She occasionally smoked marijuana for a few days straight, she perfected the art of flirtation and tease, she was well known for her posing ability and talent at being standoffish, and there were not many people who loved sex more than she did. When a connection was established, and the particulars worked out, Victoria was as good or better at her craft as any adult film legend, and when she was with someone, which wasn't as often as many people thought, she made him feel as though he was the greatest man ever born on Earth. However, like many women, Victoria sometimes made big mistakes judging men. Her biggest error in character judgment had come a couple of years ago, when she was at a big-budget club on the South Beach strip and met Martin Martinez, long considered one of the best looking men in the area, judging from his popularity with the ladies. Victoria was hooked almost immediately, except she and Martin never got to know each other, and after several months of sexual bliss and moving in together, things began to change for the worse.

A very proud woman, she had already been in a situation at home in New York when she was young with an older man named Frederico, who mistreated her but was just good enough to her to be able to take advantage of her inexperience and vulnerability. And even though Victoria loved Frederico, she and Martin tried to make a new life together. In the back of her mind, though, Victoria still cared for Frederico, and when Martin disrespected Victoria for what would be the final time, she picked up her things and she left, driving all the way to New York in one day. Hurt like never before, she immersed herself in trying to find employment and worked at TapTown through a family friend to give herself something to do in the meantime. Of course, when Frederico found out she had returned, the phone calls would not stop. In fact, when all of her exes found out she had returned, they tried to rekindle their relationship with her. It didn't work for most, but it worked for Frederico. Despite being in and out of the New York City penal system, Frederico always managed to say the right thing at the right time; and Victoria always fell for it.

Victoria took a shower and ate some leftover Chinese food she had ordered a few nights before. As she lay on her bed afterward, still a bit scared of being alone and staring at the ceiling, she wondered if she would ever meet a man she could truly count on.

Chapter 19

Zack couldn't have been more hung over on Sunday if he tried. His eyes opened, bloodshot, at 12:57 p.m., three minutes to game time. He rolled over, searching on the floor for the remote control, knocking over the plastic iced tea bottle along the way. It rolled under the futon and hit the wall behind it. "Aw fuck it, I'll get it when I clean up," Zack said to himself, picking up the remote and putting the game on. He sat upright and stared at the screen, oblivious. "Gotta stop staying out so late, I'm getting older." He shrugged with a laugh while knowing he wasn't going to take his own advice anytime soon. He called his parents to check in with them and make sure they were OK so he wouldn't have to call later on and interrupt his relaxation day. They were fine and both in the mood to talk a lot.

Zack worked his way through the next 45 minutes the best he could. He ordered the pizza he had craved for so long and ate half of it. He didn't feel very well and started to get a headache that had nothing to do with the night before. He felt nervous and anxious and as if he was losing control of his thoughts. He was always happy on the outside and bitter and angry deep down, but he always kept it in check. Everyone was probably like he was, Zack thought. Until now. He felt like he would explode and that at any moment the emotions he had kept bottled in for so many years would rise to the surface. It felt strange to be that way, he thought, and it was so sudden that he had no idea how to deal with it. He didn't say a word all day long after the conversation with his parents and fell asleep about 8:30 p.m.

When he woke up, it was Monday morning, Sept. 20, at 7:30p.m. Zack had forgotten to set the alarm, and, in a panic, he jumped in the shower for two minutes, brushed his teeth, put on his clothes, and ran out the door to the subway. He didn't get to work until 9:15, 45 minutes late. Zack worked on State Street in a high-rise building on the 24th floor. His desk had a clear view of the World Trade Center. But none of this mattered today. The boss, James Jackson, associate publisher of The Executive Recruiter, was a stickler for punctuality, and after allowing Zack to leave early last Tuesday for his trip to Texas, the last thing he wanted to see was Zack arriving this late. Zack was sweating on this somewhat brisk autumn morning in lower Manhattan, still feeling terrible, when he sat down at his desk, waiting for the inevitable. Jackson soon walked over to him.

"Hey Zack, how was the trip?" Jackson asked with a stern look on his face.

"It was fantastic, thanks. It's always good to see the parents." Zack had a sheepish grin.

"Well, glad you made it back. I've got to run to a meeting but I have something for you to do for me later today that may take a while. I hope you have some to spare." Jackson stared at Zack for a second, and then he walked off. Zack knew he would be at work past the normal 5:30 today, probably well past it. It sucked, he thought, but he was late, so he had to deal with the consequences.

Zack was feeling even more sick by 10 a.m. He knew he hadn't gotten enough rest, and combined with being rushed in the morning, and a cold front running through downtown, it wasn't a good day to be Zack. He had taken some aspirin he had in his desk, but a few hours later, he felt even worse. So he ate lunch at his desk rather than walk around and be even more fatigued than he already was. He got a tuna sandwich from the company cafeteria on the same floor. It wasn't very good. It had celery and carrots in it. Zack only liked tuna the way his mom made it: with nothing but mayo. But he managed to eat the bulk of it because he was hungry.

At about 2 p.m., Jackson called Zack in to his office and told him about a new sales pitch for a major client that he needed him to work on that the executive vice presidents wanted to see on Wednesday. He wanted a draft of a proposal on his desk at 10 on Tuesday morning. "10 A.M. TUESDAY??" Zack thought. "You've got to be kidding!" Jackson wasn't kidding. Zack went back to his desk, sat down, put his head in his hands, loosened his tie, and started to formulate the proposal. It was 3 p.m.

At 5, he was finally in a groove, and even though he had to work late, he knew what to do with the proposal and how it was to look. The problem was that he felt like hell. It was as if whatever he did to make himself feel better - eat something, take an aspirin - made it worse. His eyes felt heavy and his body felt like he had the flu. He struggled to continue working on the proposal. It was 6 p.m. and everyone was leaving. Soon, Zack was alone and it was dark outside. It was 7:30. He fired himself up and decided he was going to finish the damn proposal if it was the last thing he ever did, and he did nothing but concentrate on it. Finally, at 10:30 p.m., he was satisfied with what he produced; it was a 10-page presentation with graphics that he was certain Jackson would feel confident giving to the higher-ups. Zack was relieved that he met the challenge and left a copy on Jackson's chair, in addition to emailing him the file. But he was angry that he wasn't going to get home until midnight at this rate, only to have to get up and do it all over again tomorrow. And it would be nice if he got to work on time, too. So he put on his jacket and picked up his laptop bag he left at the office over the weekend, put his cell phone in it, and left.

Nobody was at the front desk when Zack walked out onto State Street. He was nearly bowled completely over by the initial gust of wind coming off the harbor. It was unbelievable, like nothing he'd ever experienced. The wind near the Staten Island Ferry was always a big factor, but this was ridiculous. He walked into the wind toward the subway station, slowly, looking like he was plodding through the desert sand. He couldn't see in front of him but he thought he knew the way, so he just looked at the sidewalk and kept going into the wind. Nobody was around at all, no cars, no people, no nothing. New York is the city that never sleeps, but not downtown near Bowling Green late at night.

The wind began to pick up even more, and Zack found himself being moved further and further to his left toward the concrete wall he had been walking alongside. By a few minutes later, he was about 50 yards from the subway station, but the wind was even stronger. It had to be 65 to 70 miles per hour, maybe more. Zack eventually straddled the wall of a building to help keep his balance, still looking down. He was becoming disoriented and unable to tell where he was, so he stopped and decided to wait and rest in the wind until he could get his bearings about him. He noticed a door a few feet ahead so he struggled to get to it and decided he would hold onto the knob for a second and rest. He leaned his body face forward into the door and grabbed the knob to hold on. But suddenly the door opened and the wind threw Zack and his laptop bag into a dark space. Zack fell but quickly got up and picked up his bag. He barely saw it by the faint light coming through the door. Without warning, the wind reversed course and slammed the door shut with a powerful, vibrating, and frightening thud. As soon as it happened, there was complete darkness and nearly complete silence. Only the faint sound of the howling wind outside was audible. Zack was terrified.

He felt around in a panic for the doorknob but he couldn't find it. He was locked into a building from the inside. He had no idea what building it was because he was lost on the street outside from having to look down the whole way. He immediately began pounding on the door in the darkness, yelling for help a few times before he realized that he sounded like a victim in a slasher movie and he stopped. He sat down, hearing a bit of a squeak when he did. He didn't know if he made a rat scurry away or whether he was already hallucinating.

"Where the fuck am I? Oh my God!" he thought as he stayed as still as possible and held the laptop bag between his legs as he sat upright on the cold concrete floor. Afraid to move, he sat there in the quiet and pitch-black darkness, pondering his next move and trying to stay calm.

Chapter 20

Zack sat in the darkness for several minutes, completely still. His right shoulder was leaning against the door he couldn't open and his left arm clutched his laptop bag. Inside the bag were a notepad and pen, a magazine, and his cell phone. He was petrified at not knowing how far to his left the vast darkness extended. There could have been another door a foot away but he couldn't see anything so he had no idea, and that frightened him even more. After a few more minutes in silence, he had calmed enough to begin to think.

"I'm not in a damned haunted house," he thought, realizing he could just call 911 and have the police track his phone to his location and let him out of whatever building he was in. Of course, he opened the phone and had no reception. But he did have some light. The cell phone panel was lit in a bright green, so Zack slowly held it up. A wall was a few feet in front of him. Turning the phone to the left, another door was illuminated about six feet away. Zack gathered himself, and rose with his bag and walked toward the door, holding the phone in front of him like a gun. He tried the door. This time, it opened, but it led to another pitch-black area. Not stepping through because he didn't know if there were stairs or some beast waiting for him, he slowly moved the phone light in position to guide him. There was a long hallway in front of him now, and he walked very slowly down the corridor. The door slammed behind him, startling him for a moment and echoing a bit. It was still silent except for his footsteps and breathing. At the end of the hallway he could see yet another door. It, too, was unlocked. When he opened this door, Zack had held the phone down. He noticed the outside of his left arm grazing something as he took a half step through the doorway. The laptop bag was on the inside of his arm, so it couldn't have been that. He slowly moved the phone light in his right hand to view what he was in contact with. Startled, he instinctively darted back in fear to his right, hitting a wall and sliding down onto the seat of his pants. Moving the light back toward what had frightened him, Zack gradually saw a huge, intimidating concrete statue of what appeared to be some type of warrior. It had to be at least seven feet tall. Standing up and moving the phone to the right, Zack noticed that he was in a large room with display cases. The dots began to connect. He thought he must have walked north on State Street in the wind and been knocked into a side door of the Indian Museum, which was a block and a half from his office building. This realization only made him a bit less frightened, however, and he walked very slowly into the room he was in, looking back twice at the huge statue that was staring directly at him as he crept away from it. Shining the phone into a few of the cases, he could see some artifacts and some descriptions of where they came from. It was 11:10 p.m. on Monday, and

Zack was taking a solo tour of a museum he was locked inside of. He couldn't believe it. He just couldn't believe it. He called out, but not too loudly, for help to find out if a security guard was there. He got no response. He had never been to this museum, and he knew that it took up an entire block of space. So he knew that he was in a small part of a vast network of rooms and floors. The light showed a couple of hallways in the distance and a door to the left between two display cases against the wall. A bit afraid to venture into the pitch-black corridors again, Zack decided to go through the door. It turned out to be an office of some type.

Zack felt a bit relieved to be in a space that looked familiar. With the phone light, he found a light switch just inside the doorway and flicked it on. It was a decent-sized space, about 30 feet wide and the same distance in front of him. There were two long tables with various books on them and some metal folding chairs, several filing cabinets, a water cooler, and a large desk with some papers strewn about it. There was a phone on the desk. Zack rushed over to it, only to find that it was a rotary phone with one option on it, apparently an interoffice phone only. That couldn't be any dumber, he thought, also assuming that this was a library of sorts, or a research room. He sat down and put the laptop bag and the phone on one of the tables, and exhaled. What a night, he thought. His adventure had caused him to forget just how much worse he was feeling than he did at the office earlier that evening. He was sweating profusely, his eyes were even heavier, and he had a massive headache. He attributed it to being hungry – he hadn't eaten since noon – and completely stressed out over being where he was and having to do that proposal. Now he was concerned about how the hell he was going to get out of this museum. He lived at least an hour away by train and had to be at work at 8:30 Tuesday morning. He had to be proactive and get the hell out of there. Now. Zack grabbed the laptop bag and got up from the table. Reaching for the cell phone, he noticed a book on the table. It was titled *"Sacred Chants of the American Indian: Myths, Mantras, and Monsters."* Zack thought he may as well get something out of this random visit that wasn't his choice, and he stashed the book in his bag, walked to the door, flicked the light off, and went back into the display case room with his phone. He could have left the office light on to help guide him, but for some reason, Zack didn't think that was a good idea.

Passing the giant warrior statue on his way toward one of the two dark passageways in front of him, he switched the phone to his left hand and raised his right hand toward the looming figure. He gave the warrior the finger and whispered "Fuck you." Zack was obviously becoming more comfortable with his surroundings. The sweat was now beading on his forehead and his head was spinning a bit, but he had to forge ahead. The phone light guided him down the corridor he chose and in the distance, about 50 feet away, was a red light. To Zack, it was a beacon. Going toward the light, he passed a large cafeteria to his left and a few more rooms with display cases and statues. Happiness and relief swallowed Zack whole as he saw that the red light from a distance was now a sign that upon closer review read 'EXIT.' It was above a door with one of those long gold bar handles that extend across the entire length of the frame. Zack stopped and looked at it for a second or two, as if to will it to release him from bondage. He then forcefully pushed the bar and walked out of the museum. He was to the right of the main entrance, and the subway was directly in front of him, the green subway lamppost the only manmade light in the area. The wind was virtually nonexistent. Zack turned to the right and violently vomited into some shrubbery and onto the museum wall. He gathered himself, looked around, and then he gingerly walked to the train and sweated his way home.

Chapter 21

Sheriff Chris David decided to leave Farley at the office for the short drive to Apache Foods. Farley would only get in the way of progress, if there was any to be made. Nothing was found at Greg Farber's residence other than Greg Farber, some ashes on the floor, a crinkled corner of a piece of yellowish paper, and Greg's mother, Jean. There were no fingerprints of anyone other than Greg, Hank, and Jean anywhere else in the house, which made sense. Hank never let anyone come in, lest they see the broken lamps or holes he punched in the walls and get suspicious. So David was visiting the office as more of a formality, to ask about how Greg was getting along at work, the same old questions David had asked dozens of employers over the years in suicide cases. He had called ahead, and Edmund greeted him at the front doors to the company.

"Hi Sheriff David, nice to see you again," Edmund said with a handshake. The sheriff was two years younger than Edmund and Daniel and was a sophomore when the two were seniors at Rossage High School.

"Feeling's mutual, Edmund, how have you been?" replied David as the two walked to Edmund's office.

"I must admit, sheriff, I've been better," Edmund said with a nervous laugh. This was not a good time for Edmund Chandler. Having taken so much pride in bringing Greg on board, it didn't sit well with him that his hire just blew his own brains out. "Nobody here saw this coming." David asked him about Greg's duties and his relationships with the other staff. Edmund was in the middle of telling David that Greg got along well with his colleagues when Daniel walked in to join the conversation.

"Daniel Smith," the sheriff proclaimed loudly, standing to shake the CEO's hand. "You made my girlfriend so happy when you made that big catch way back when that she ended up marrying me. Now I get a chance to thank you for it." Daniel and Edmund got a big kick out of David's glee. He was always such a serious man. But once again, just thoughts of a former athlete's prowess brought back smiles to his constituents.

"Boy, that sure was a long time ago, sheriff," Daniel said. "But I remember it like it was yesterday. Still brings a smile, as it should I guess." Sheriff David and Edmund both nodded in agreement.

"Mr. Smith, I wish I was here under better circumstances," the sheriff continued.

"Yes, I couldn't believe the news when Edmund told me," Daniel said. "I felt so badly that I didn't get to speak with him while he was here." The sheriff was surprised that Daniel had not even spoken with Greg since he was hired. But Edmund informed him that Daniel had been out for a couple of months acquiring test markets for a new candy bar line.

There really wasn't much left to ask, since this was pretty much a routine visit to confirm employment and to try to get some sort of reason behind Greg's suicide. But he did well at work and didn't have any enemies. Satisfied with the meeting, the sheriff left to a round of hearty goodbyes all around, drove back to the precinct, filled out a short report, placed the sheet of paper in a manila folder and tucked it away in an old gray file cabinet under a tab that read "CLOSED".

Chapter 22

Zack barely made it through the door to his apartment before collapsing in a sea of sweat on the floor next to his futon. He was dizzy, soaked, and his head was throbbing. He crawled to the bathroom and threw up. He noticed through the fog in his mind that the vomit was a greenish-red tint. This made him feel even worse. He had no idea how he was going to get to work the next morning, and to top it all off, he got angry because he had missed a chance to go to TapTown and talk to Victoria, meaning some idiot might have worked his way in to her heart before he had an opportunity.

He toweled off his body as best he could, stopped at the refrigerator for a chug of water out of the liter bottle he had, limped back to the futon, climbed on it, grabbed the sheet like a baby, and closed his eyes. He then remembered that he needed to set the alarm, so he reached up, felt around for the switch, and flipped it to alarm mode, never opening his eyes. Zack was very sick. Deciding not to even wait until dawn to call in, he dangled his foot off the side of the futon to drag the laptop bag over to him. His cell phone was his only phone, so he cracked his eyes open a bit, fumbled around for it, dialed the number to James Jackson and left a message informing him that he was too sick to make it in and that he had several sick days left and needed to use one. Normally, Zack would come up with a wild excuse, such as a gas leak in his apartment, to get out of going to the office, but he wasn't in the mood for jokes. Closing his eyes again, Zack was able to get to sleep, but this was just the beginning of his night.

Zack was drifting between sleep mode and a kaleidoscope effect that took his mind on a trip through a new universe of color…dark color. Everything was black, deep purple, maroon, forest green, and there were noises that varied between mouse-like squeaks and vibrating human grunts dominating the background. Pictures then flashed through the sequence: insects, cells, a school of sharks, a gun, trees, human waste, and other random things Zack couldn't understand. Then, like a vortex sucking up everything in its path, it all disappeared. Zack woke up, five seconds before the alarm. He turned it off and looked around himself. He wasn't sweating any more, and the bed was dry as a bone. No headache, no queasiness. He wasn't sure what happened, but he felt fine.

"What a fucked up dream," he sighed, sitting upright on the futon. He turned on the television. Sports highlights were on. He thought to himself that it must have been the old 24-hour virus people sometimes get. But he had already called in sick and wasn't about to reverse that call. And the proposal was airtight; no way that he'd get in hot water for any part of it. It was official. Zack Williams had a day off.

Chapter 23

Zack took a shower on this glorious Tuesday and walked over to the diner for a big breakfast. He felt fantastic. He ordered three scrambled eggs, pancakes, sausage, bacon, and orange juice and ate all of it in 20 minutes. While he ate, Jackson had called him and left a voice mail stating that he got his message and hoped he would feel better. It was in a less-than-comforting monotone, but Zack didn't care. Sick days, to Zack, were to be used just like any other benefit a company provides, and he felt no guilt at all for using them. He went back to the apartment and did an hour on the elliptical machine and barely broke a sweat, took a shower, and went through his personal and work emails. It was only 10 a.m. Zack decided to do one of his favorite activities: ride the train from one end of the line to the other. He lived across the street from several train lines, but today he chose the Brooklyn train.

He got on the subway about 10:30 and rode all the way to Coney Island, passing underground through Queens, Manhattan and Brooklyn. Zack got off the train and walked across the street to the amusement park, taking a few swings at the batting cage, having a beer, and then winning a prize at the shooting gallery. Unfortunately, the only gift they were giving away was a stuffed animal. So Zack chose the bee, and left. The aquarium was open down the street, so he decided to stop by. It was only 1p.m. and he had all day and all night. Zack loved penguins, so he spent a lot of time watching them waddle around in their cold universe. He had always wished he could have a penguin for a pet and even had a couple of books about them. Oh well, it was wishful thinking, he said to himself. He looked both ways to make sure nobody was watching, and he waved to the penguins with a huge smile before walking away. Before heading back to Queens, Zack decided he better grab a quick lunch. So he got a hot dog and stood at an outdoor table and took his time, looking around at the Brooklyn locals passing by. With amusement parks and restaurants come insects, so he shooed away a fly that landed on the table. A few more stopped by, too, and then a few more. He was getting upset about it, so it was a good thing that he had finished the hot dog and was on his way.

It had been a long day already, so Zack decided he would spend the rest of it at home relaxing. He got back to his apartment around 3:15 p.m., dropped his stuffed bee on the floor, and changed into his underwear. He was watching television, a bit bored but content, when he spotted the book he stole from the museum sticking out of the laptop bag near him. He reached over and picked it up. *"Sacred Chants of the American Indian: Myths, Mantras, and Monsters,"* by Bill Freeman, was a modest, 80-page soft cover book. In the midst of Zack's experience at the museum, a pitch-black environment, a dimly lit office, and a massive and scary warrior statue looming in the distance, the book seemed like an exciting read. In Zack's apartment while he was wearing boxer shorts and sitting on the hardwood floor, with the stereo playing and sports highlights on the television, the book didn't hold as much appeal. But he thumbed through it anyway.

In the bio section, Zack read that Freeman was a renegade Apache Indian who ran away from the tribe he was a part of, secretly taking chants with him that he published for the world to see so they could find out more about the mystery of the Indian. Bill Freeman was a fake name, so that he couldn't be found. Zack figured that whoever Freeman ran away from was probably pretty pissed off about it. Then he giggled and kept reading. He saw a few pieces on the Native American and his relationship to Black Americans, stories about peace pipes and their true uses, and then came upon a section devoted to chants and which ones were true and which weren't. Zack wasn't superstitious at all, since he wasn't the type to believe in abstract things other than God. So he started reading some of the chants, including one that combined with a potion, would supposedly turn a person into a deer. He thought to himself that if that one worked, he would go down the hall and stomp the shit out of his neighbor, who was never polite to him. Of course, it didn't work. He laughed, shrugged and looked up at the television. A commercial for bug spray was on; the one where the roaches explode after the housewife sprays them. Zack always liked that one. He cracked a smile and went back to perusing the book. The next chapter was about the Flying Chant, which was supposed to allow the person who ate or drank some sort of mixture to recite the words and morph into whatever flying being was included in the potion. There was more about intentions and effects, but Zack just skimmed through the next few paragraphs, since he wasn't taking any of what he was reading very seriously. Incredibly stupid shit, Zack thought, just incredibly stupid. Amused by the fact that he was sitting Indian style on the floor, Zack leaned back with a hearty laugh and looked at the chant. With arms extended, the potion eater was supposed to recite:

MUNCHAKA DUNAGI
LEMAKI MUNCHAK

Zack obviously had no idea what this meant, and the book didn't go into translations. He wasn't going to make the effort to find it, either. So, having fun with the book, he followed the directions and stood up, extended his arms out from his sides with palms facing up, closed his eyes, and belted it out: "Munchaka dunagi lemaki munchak!" Nothing happened.

Zack said in a low tone, "Figures. That shit was never gonna work anyw-"

Suddenly, Zack grabbed at his stomach in excruciating, intense pain and screamed as if he were being repeatedly shot in the same place or stabbed all over his body. He started to convulse and vomit a thick, milky, whitish-green fluid. His eyes felt like they were going to pop out of his head. He grabbed his head and continued to scream at the top of his lungs. It was a work day, and nobody was around to hear him. He fell to the floor with a giant thud in a heap and felt his own chest caving in and his bones creaking and shifting like they were shrinking, and without warning a shriek went through his head, a high-pitched noise like the one the subway wheels would make when it would come in to certain stations and rub against the tracks. He passed out for a few seconds, completely disoriented and detached from reality.

When Zack opened his eyes, he closed them almost immediately. It was as if he saw 20 of the same thing out of each eye. He felt like he had taken every drug imaginable and was invincible, yet confined. He tried opening his eyes again, and he realized that he was indeed seeing several of the same images out of his eyes. Gradually the images became one for him, but he was confused. He tried to stand up but couldn't. Looking down to see what was wrong with his legs, he screamed with such anguish and frightened surprise that he began to wail in fear. He tried to lift his arms to see them, and it was the same effect. Both his arms and legs looked like tentacles of some sort. He didn't even notice anything about his surroundings until just then, when he looked to the right and saw an unbelievably large object, maybe 500 times his size. It was his stereo speaker. He looked around timidly and realized that his apartment had become nearly a thousand times bigger than it was. Still wailing and in constant fear, he tried to think things through. The only thought running through his mind over and over was that he had no idea what had happened to him or his apartment or his arms and legs. He couldn't stand up, and everything was so much bigger. Was it like that outside? How would he ever be normal again? Zack tried to run but couldn't. In an attempt to push further off his legs to try to walk faster, his entire body rose off the ground like a helicopter and he felt pressure and pain coming from his back. "Sweet Jesus, am I flying around this apartment?" an astonished and pained Zack wondered. After getting past the initial shock of what was going on, the answer to that question was simply, 'Yes.'

33-year-old Zachary Williams of New York had recited an Indian myth chant out of a book he stole from a museum he got blown into off the street and turned into a fly. He had no idea how and didn't think he would ever figure it out. He didn't remember eating any kind of potion in his life; all he remembered eating the last two days was a bad tuna sandwich and half a pizza. And he had no idea how to become himself again. None. He sobbed inside for what seemed an eternity, not knowing if he would ever be able to contact his family and friends again. He was too small to do anything but barely fly. He couldn't do anything else. Not anything.

Zack calmed himself enough and managed to get himself up to the futon. To his right was a full length mirror attached to his closet. Glancing over, he screamed in fright. His eyes were his own but the rest of him was a fly. Devastated and feeling hopeless, he looked over the edge of the futon and was frightened that if he tried to fly down, he would fall and kill himself. Confused and hurt beyond belief, he sat there, a fly on a futon, and cried again, nonstop, for two hours, completely isolated and wondering, once again, if he would ever be human again.

Chapter 24

The crying and stunned sadness finally subsided for Zack Williams. Trying to gather himself now and deal with his reality, which now meant being a hated household pest, Zack came to a scary conclusion about his situation. He would have to recite the chant again and hope that it turned him back into his old self. If it didn't, he was finished. The problem was finding a way to do it.

Zack didn't remember the chant, and the book, still on the floor, was open to the page the chant was on. But as a fly, Zack couldn't see the writing from his perch on the edge of the futon. He would have to try to fly to the book. He breathed out heavily and lifted with his legs and arched his back to make his wings flap. He managed to fly straight up, off the futon, and then ventured outward over the floor below him. It looked like the distance the coyote faced when he always fell off a cliff chasing the roadrunner. He managed to steady his flight and hover above the book. He could see the chant in print now, and he breathed in and said it firmly, hoping beyond his wildest dreams that it would work. "Munchaka dunagi lemaki munchak."

Zack fell to the floor in a monstrous heap, hitting his leg on a table next to the book he slammed into from above. He had a slight glaze of a foreign substance on parts of him and his boxer shorts were damp but not soaked. If he were in public, people would probably have thought he had just finished jogging. He noticed his foot was resting in a pool of the vomit he expelled when he turned into a fly. He pulled the book out from under his body, feeling both disoriented and incredibly thankful. He sat up and turned off the stereo, then collapsed again to the floor, his entire body having spread out like a child before starting to make snow angels. Staring at the ceiling, he wondered what the hell had just happened to him. Then he struggled to get up and walked toward the restroom to take a shower, dazed and confused.

As the water cascaded over his head, Zack began to slowly realize what this episode meant for his future days if this chant was something that would regularly become a part of his routine. If he could learn to fly very well, anything would be possible, he thought to himself. He could go anywhere he wanted as long as a door was open, a window, a crevice. He tried to quash the thoughts and make this an isolated incident that frightened the hell out of him and showed him that there was no way he should repeat it ever again. It wasn't working at all. Buildup of excitement was unavoidable in a man like Zack. He was lonely, angry, frustrated, and had settled into a routine that was becoming boring and lifeless. What just happened to him gave him a feeling of excitement he had never felt before and made him think he could have unprecedented access to things he may never have otherwise.

For a minute, he knew just how insane he sounded, how ridiculously insane he must have been to even think that for a second he could actually live his life with this newfound phenomenon and be happy. He knew that a fly swatter, a frog, a shoe, or anything else he ever used to rid himself of a fly could easily be his downfall if he even made a halfhearted attempt to leave his apartment as anything other than Zack Williams, human male. Always the practical thinker, Zack knew that this was a one-shot deal that was weird but not reality. It couldn't be reality. He decided to be a man of action.

Zack got out of the shower, dried off, put on some clothes, cleaned up the vomit, walked firmly over to the book of chants, closed it, walked out of his front door and down the hallway, and deposited it into the garbage shaft. He would never remember the chant. It was over and done with, and it was time to get back to work Wednesday and earn a living.

Chapter 25

"What the hell is this shit??"

This loud question from James Jackson is the first thing Zack heard when he got to the office on Wednesday. "This fucking proposal is missing an entire section it needs! The VPs are gonna look at me like I'm damn near crazy!"

"What section is missing?" Zack asked calmly.

"Man, just get the hell out of my office."

Zack turned and walked out, went back to his desk, and sat there with his hands folded. Everybody in the office stared at him as he was walking back, and he was so embarrassed that he sat motionless, not quite sure what to do next, engulfed with anger at Jackson. Zack had a great record of achievement at work, was one of the top five salespersons at the company in the year he had been there, and was respected and liked by his colleagues and clients. He saw no reason for this outburst and was trying his best to control his emotions. Unfortunately, this had not been the first time Jackson had tried berated or downgraded Zack in front of others.

At last year's Christmas party, Jackson asked Zack how the holiday parties were at companies in Texas. Zack said they were pretty much the same, just a bit warmer outside. As his colleagues standing around at the time laughed warmly, Jackson said "Oh, I figured they would lynch you from the Christmas tree as a practical joke." The awkward silence was deafening and Zack had an incredulous look on his face, staring at Jackson in disbelief. It was one thing for him to say something so patently offensive, Zack thought; it was another entirely to say something like that and also be a black man. Zack never forgave him for it, primarily because Jackson never apologized. Now, after several other smaller run-ins, this was the last straw. He started to feel nauseous again and his headache returned within a half hour.

Zack waited until Jackson went to lunch and then told Martha, the group secretary, that he didn't feel well and would be back tomorrow. He looked so sad that Martha offered him a piece of candy, the type Grandma Helen used to give him when he would visit, a red and white swirl candy. But his sad look was an act; Zack didn't want anyone to see how angry he truly was. He gathered his things and left the office, walking past the Indian museum and up to some benches in the park near the subway station. He sat down with a sandwich, alone, looking nowhere in particular. As if on cue, Jackson then walked by with a VP at the company, Jim Sheridan. The bigwig stopped when he noticed Zack on the bench.

"Zack, we met at the Christmas party last year but I wanted to say hello again," Sheridan said with a handshake as Zack stood up to acknowledge him. Jackson said nothing. "You've been doing good work, keep it up! Glad to have you aboard."

"Thanks a lot for the kind words, Mr. Sheridan, I really appreciate it. Glad to be here," Zack replied. As the two left Zack at the bench, Jackson glanced back at him with disgust. Zack looked away, thinking to himself, "Wait until that bastard finds out from Martha that I'm not coming back today." He couldn't eat his sandwich because he was so mad. So he went home.

While Zack was on the train, Jackson left him a voicemail on his phone. Zack checked it when he got home. "Zack, this is James. When you get in tomorrow, we're going to have a serious discussion on your status at this company. I don't care what Sheridan said to you today, I have some issues we need to discuss immediately. And quite frankly, I'm the one who will be doing most of the talking. Come to my office as soon as you get in, preferably on time." Zack couldn't take it any more. He was only late on Monday and one other time a few months ago when the trains were flooded in Queens during a storm. Everyone was late that day. He sat on the futon, enraged, rocking back and forth with his head in his hands. He calmed himself enough to try to eat some soup. He was hungry and it was just 3 p.m. But he couldn't do it. After two sips, he pushed the bowl away from him and looked down. He didn't know what to do. His professional life was being completely ruined by Jackson, and it was affecting his personal life and making him physically ill. He tried to lie down and put a cold towel on his head to calm himself but it was to no avail. He knew that tomorrow Jackson was going to try to rip him a new one, probably embarrass him again, and give him more work than was reasonable. On top of that, yesterday he had literally the day from hell; and he couldn't tell anyone about it without them trying to get him committed.

Zack leapt from the futon, put on his shoes, and ran down to the basement from his apartment. He walked briskly down the long corridor of the poorly lit lower level and opened the door to the trash chute. There was an extraordinary amount of garbage piled up from the 10 floors of residents on his side of the building. In a panic, he began to rummage with his bare hands through the trash looking for what he had to have. Pulling out and moving out of his way everything from spaghetti to water bottles to empty TV dinner trays to fully occupied roach motels, Zack finally saw what he was seeking. It was the chant book. He brought it upstairs with him, and then he washed his hands of the refuse they had collected in the basement.

Chapter 26

Zack sat on his futon. It was 4 p.m. He was staring at the chant book on the table. He knew that he was about to go to a place he couldn't turn back from. He turned to the same section that got him into this mess. It said that the person who had ingested the potion would be able to use the chant for the rest of his life and cautioned that no matter what they did, if they were not the person who made the potion, then they were at the mercy of the person who did. If that person didn't make the potion with good intentions, then the person who actually ingested it was doomed to a life of anguish, no matter how hard they tried to live happily. It also said that the chant had to be stated word for word or it wouldn't work. Zack somehow mustered a laugh at reading the entire paragraph, despite having actually morphed into a winged, sad, and part-human, part-fly beast just a day ago.

"This Freeman guy must be crazy," Zack thought. "Then again, I was a fucking fly yesterday, so maybe I should pay attention. Besides, where was this so-called potion? In a pizza? A tuna sandwich? This is ridiculous."

Zack had always had a different way of viewing things. There was a saying about not letting the small things bother someone. Zack was the opposite. He thought that it was the big things, the things out of people's control, that shouldn't concern them. It was the smaller things, the bothersome stuff that made everyday life more tempestuous and excruciating, which got to Zack. The president could cut healthcare options for the elderly, and Zack would be upset about it. But if someone left a piece of gum in a seat at the movie theater and Zack sat down on it, he would want to find the perpetrator and break his back. Knowing that he could say his chant and go from human to "fly thingy," as he thought to himself, was revolutionary and could help him solve all of his personal issues and get rid of all of his inner demons. His spirituality and connection with God that he had so valued as the only abstract part of his life that mattered was suddenly becoming blurry. How could Zack possibly have that intimate level of personal faith and submit to what his mind was now generating? There wasn't a way in hell that God would approve of what he was pondering. It would end up breaking every commandment and ensuring Zack an eternity of boiling in the hot lava cave that he had always envisioned hell to be. Had Zack's faith been erased completely in the lone moment of metamorphosis he had experienced? It seemed so, as he plotted his next move for the evening.

Zack got a tip at a bar from a thug and used it to illegally purchase a small-caliber gun, a .22, for protection when he first arrived in New York. The serial number was nowhere to be found, and he kept it under his sink behind some old magazines. Zack retrieved the gun and put it in his pocket.

He had on loose-fitting jeans. To test his theory and to try to get adjusted to the pain that the chant caused, he said it and went into the same convulsions he had the other time, but they didn't last as long. He vomited much less and, because it wasn't a surprise to him this time, it didn't hurt as much. He flew around the apartment and gradually began to gain control of his flight paths and was learning how to land on different surfaces, the grimy top of his window sill, his table, the futon, and the hardwood floors. He had turned on the air conditioner because he was hot when he had come back from the trash chute. The air blew him straight into one of his walls when he was flying around, but it didn't hurt him. He knew he would need to be careful, as there were many pitfalls ahead of him that could end his existence, and the one thing he didn't know was whether his death as a mutant would result in his death as Zack, or even if it would automatically return him to human form. This frightened Zack immeasurably, but not enough to stop carrying out what he was planning.

Having gained the courage he needed, Zack said the chant and was human again. He went to the restroom and cut off all of his hair. He liked the bald look and admired it in the mirror for a while then applied sheen to make his head shinier. He proceeded to shave all of his body hair off, from head to toe. It didn't take him very long, as he didn't have any significant body hair other than under his arms and around his genitals. He went to his closet and put on a tight-fitting, black, cold-weather workout outfit he had gotten when he went to Texas, the kind that football players wear when they work out. He looked like a speed skater, covered from head to toe. The outfit had a space in it at stomach level to fit a few objects and snap shut. Presumably, it was for a portable music device or some athletic gear. Zack dated a surgeon's assistant when he first got to New York. She had left a surgical mask and a few pairs of surgical gloves at his place. He put the mask and a pair of gloves, as well as the loaded gun, in the suit space. He had on tight rubber shoes that fit perfectly over the bottom of the workout gear. They were similar to the shoes sprinters wear, except the bottom grooves were worn out so there was no traction. They were about a size too large, so Zack stuffed some tissue paper in the front of each shoe so they would fit comfortably. He had forgotten where he got them, probably in Texas. Nothing could get out of his outfit and nothing could get in. Then he went back to the futon, sat down, and thumbed through his rolodex for James Jackson's address.

Chapter 27

James Jackson had been on the fast track all his life, and nothing was going to stop him. A quick learner and type A personality, Jackson graduated from Morton College, a historically black college in South Carolina, with a degree in advertising and then put in 30 years of strong employment at several Fortune 500 firms, rising each step of the way. He got married and had a son, but after his divorce two years later, the family remained down south and Jackson moved to New York.

When he was hired as associate VP at The Executive Publisher, Jackson threw himself a party and had some of the famous people in entertainment that he had met along his career path attend. He was a hard worker, but he wouldn't let anyone get in his way, especially not another man of color. He didn't believe in affirmative action, thinking that it was hard work that got everyone who was ever a success to the top. He didn't believe at all that bad luck or timing or circumstance or bias ever played a part in anyone's life. "If you can't make it in life," Jackson once said to Zack, "then it's your damn fault, not anyone else's." He said anything he wanted to say, usually without regard to who was around. It was this attribute and his attitudes that made for a big clash of personality with Zack. Jackson hadn't hired Zack, having arrived at the company just after Zack came on board. He didn't think Zack worked hard enough, and Jackson told Zack as much within a month after he got there. Zack told him that he was just efficient, and while it may seem like he isn't busting his tail, his track record in the business should tell Jackson that he need not worry that Zack is slacking. Jackson wasn't buying it; and there was no direction they could go together at the crossroads. They hated each other, and that was it.

However, Zack never gave anyone an indication that he hated Jackson. Zack always moped around and looked despondent after one of their arguments. Meanwhile, Jackson would stomp around the office yelling, making no secret of his disdain for Zack or anyone else who he thought wasn't up to par. Zack was well-liked by everyone else at the company, including higher-ups like Sheridan, which made it even tougher for him to take Jackson's berating. It was as if the bigwigs didn't see or pay attention to the obvious abuse Jackson was inflicting on Zack, he thought. And Zack wasn't the only employee Jackson seemingly had it in for. He had cursed out a mailroom employee, another sales rep, and an intern for things that turned out to be nonsense. The intern screamed that Jackson was crazy in front of the rest of the staff and quit a few days after she started. Zack's colleague, Lisa Martino, was an outspoken Italian lady from the Bronx. She had a major run-in with Jackson during which he told her that she should be at home cooking some pasta for a mob capo. Stunned, she turned and walked out in tears and apparently was never going to come back. But she did, and she wasn't alone. Instead of going to human resources, she returned with a huge muscleman the day after the incident. He threatened to kill Jackson, using various racial epithets to help him express his feelings. It took three security guards to get him out of the building. The mailroom employee, Randy, was from East New York in Brooklyn. He had told several people, more than once, that if he saw Jackson out on the street that he would cut his throat. And everyone believed him. Zack hadn't forgotten about any of these disputes and knew that there would be no shortage of suspects if James Jackson had an unfortunate accident. Zack opened the window in his apartment about six inches. That small space would serve as the new front door for Zack's soon-to-be partner in crime; and true to his sense of humor, he nicknamed his mutated other half, Buzz.

Zack asked himself why he couldn't just find another job. But he wasn't going out like that. He had left jobs before because he didn't like his boss or the pay wasn't right. He loved his job now and was good at it. And he wasn't going to let Jackson ruin his career. In fact, Jackson was driving him out of his mind. At this point, Zack's career was the only thing keeping him sane. Zack reminded himself that he wasn't the only one who was being tormented by Jackson, so he'd act for all of the victims of Jackson's venom. And he'd act now.

Chapter 28

Zack had everything he needed.

"Munchaka dunagi lemaki munchak," he said. Within 15 seconds, he was Buzz. Flying out of the window space, Buzz guided himself toward the subway station and flew into it. He cracked a smile when he realized he could get a free ride from now on if he really wanted to. He navigated all the way to the subway platform and waited, resting on a wall. He was amazed at how he could just sit on a wall or ceiling and not fall. The train came roaring in. The tunnel wind the train created was reminiscent at times of Zack's experience when he was blown into the museum, but it felt good, even therapeutic, now. As the subway doors opened, Buzz flew in and landed on a pole. It was rush hour, but since he was going into Manhattan, the train wasn't crowded. Thrilled, he looked around at all of the giant people riding to the city who didn't remotely notice him. He drifted to sleep with the rocking of the train, just as he did when human.

About 20 minutes later, he flew off the train at Lexington Avenue and worked his way up to street level. Jackson lived near Lexington and 69th in an expensive one-bedroom apartment overlooking the street. Zack had been there once before, for a dinner party the sales staff was invited to. Jackson had said all of two words to him during the entire three-hour time period.

Buzz flew up to the third floor and looked into a window. He spotted Jackson seated in a leather chair watching television, laughing heartily, with a glass of wine next to him on a small table. He was still wearing his work clothes, even though it was nearly 6:30 p.m. Buzz thought about how much he truly hated Jackson. There was no opening through which he could enter, so he flew down to the ground level and went into the front door past the clueless doorman and up the staircase. Looking and hovering around the front door, he noticed that he was making actual buzzing sounds. How appropriate, he thought. Buzz noticed that there was a small enough space for him to get in through the mail slot. He managed his way through it and flew directly to where Jackson was sitting, resting himself on the couch behind Jackson to gather his thoughts. It was nearly Zack's time to rid himself of a problem that was ruining his quality of life. For someone else, it was a minor issue. For Zack, it was a major factor in his unhappiness.

Buzz flew over to Jackson's bathroom, which was around a corner and down a hallway. He landed on the floor, and said his chant, quietly. He was human again, a bit damp, but had everything on, and in the right place. Relieved, he pulled out the gun, put on the surgical mask and gloves, walked out of the bathroom quietly, and strolled straight over to an absolutely stunned Jackson, who stood up from his chair and yelled, "Zack! What the fuck are you doing in my apartment??" Giving no reply, Zack shot him in his left leg below the knee. Forgetting that Jackson would scream in pain and make a lot of noise, Zack shot him again in the chest, killing him instantly as he fell to the floor on his back with a giant thud. He had planned to toy with Jackson a bit, but he had to abandon that part of the evening. Then he also realized that the gun made noise and would probably attract someone any minute. Discouraged with himself for forgetting these obviously important factors, he shook his head. He then acted quickly, dragging Jackson into an open area of the apartment and disrobing him. Blood was everywhere. Zack stopped for a second and looked at it in disbelief. Strangely, it didn't bother him that much. He had seen much worse in the movies. He balled Jackson's clothes up and angrily threw them as hard as he could to the other side of the room, and left Jackson there to bleed all over the place.

Zack went looking for something to cut with and found it in a heavy and pristine hatchet in Jackson's closet. He remembered it as actually being an award given by an advertising association for being able to, as it said on the handle, "cut through the forest of rejection and clear an opening to sales success." Dumb as hell, Zack said to himself, but thank goodness Jackson had won the award.

Zack dragged the all-gold hatchet into the room where Jackson lay. He raised the hatchet and lowered the boom straight into Jackson's left leg just below the knee. Blood spewed out onto the wall and hardwood floor beneath. The bones popped out looking completely white, a stunning contrast to the dark outer skin and reddish-orange flesh inside. Repeating the effort on the other side with cold efficiency, Zack then picked up the lower halves of Jackson's legs and, extending them from his own body so as to not let them bleed on him, carried them to one of the bedroom closets. He placed each naked leg into a brown dress shoe and placed them in front of the door way. The scene was made to look like Jackson was stepping out of his bedroom with just his legs. Zack went back and chopped Jackson's arms off at the shoulder, attaching one by the hand to his front door and the other to a water knob in his bathtub. There was no meaning to any of this. Zack just thought all of the scenarios would look funny. He dragged the torso, with head and thighs still attached, to the kitchen and propped it in a chair at the table. He walked over to the cabinet, prepared a bowl of cereal with milk, and put it in front of the body on the table. He then slowly leaned the torso forward and put Jackson's dead head into the bowl. Zack got a knife from a drawer next to the refrigerator, walked back to the table, and, reaching under Jackson's angled head, took one clean backward slice across Jackson's throat, a bloodletting he had recalled seeing on a documentary about killing cows at the slaughterhouse before they went to the fast-food joints. Zack didn't care about a blood trail in the apartment. All he wanted was to humiliate Jackson as much as possible.

Thinking to himself that the mission was accomplished, he walked over and opened the window in the living room, moved into an open area, put the gun, mask and gloves in his suit compartment, repeated the chant, and flew out of Jackson's apartment. Buzz returned to the subway for a ride home, unnoticed.

Chapter 29

The train trip was tough for Buzz. The subway cars were more crowded, and he had a few close calls with people rushing in to the train at certain stops. He remembered that he could relax on the ceiling, so he got himself to the top and stayed there until he got to Kew Gardens, flew off and carefully hovered above the crowd and went home, returning through the window from where he departed.

He chanted and collapsed to the floor as Zack, exhausted with both fear and excitement. His thoughts were racing. "What have I just done?" he asked himself. What he had done was kill a man, his boss, brutally, with malice and forethought. He chopped Jackson up and left him there for the authorities to find and for his family to sob over. Zack removed the gun, mask, and gloves from his outfit, which was covered in Jackson's blood. Thinking that authorities could end up at his place during an investigation, he wondered how he would wash and hide the outfit if he needed to. Zack, becoming increasingly worried, decided that he would need a place outside of his apartment to store the items. For some reason, it had never crossed his mind before he killed Jackson. Subconsciously, he knew that he would probably need them a second time. He put the mask, gloves and gun under the sink and folded the outfit and put it down next to the futon until he could decide what to do with it. He then swept up all of the hair he shaved off earlier and put it in the trash, and got in the shower.

Standing under the water once again, Zack was in a daze. He was a killer. A killer! He had actually just killed a man. Everything that had ever happened to him, being ridiculed as a teen for nothing despite excelling with his classmates, being berated by his bosses, dumped and deceived by his girlfriends, surpassed in social or economic status by colleagues who weren't as smart as he was or by strangers he overheard at a bar or restaurant, feeling disrespected, all the stories his family had told him that made him upset, it had all built rage within him that he let out that evening. He killed someone. "Buzz, what the fuck have you done?" he asked himself over and over.

Drying himself off, Zack sat naked on the futon, staring over at the bloody clothing. He decided to abandon his paranoia and wash the outfit in the industrial washer that nobody used in the basement laundry room. In about 20 minutes, the outfit was cleaned and he brought it back to his apartment and hung it up to dry in his bathroom. It was 10 p.m. Zack went to sleep. It had been a long day.

Chapter 30

Zack arrived at the office the next morning to the usual banter. As always, he said a few hellos before sitting down at his desk. He arrived at about 8:20 a.m., 10 minutes early, and was calmer than he thought he would be, but he made an effort to look a bit downcast, because everyone knew that Jackson wanted to see him in his office, first thing. Inside, Zack couldn't help but laugh like the proverbial mad scientist, knowing that Jackson would not be in the office today…or ever again. He started to work on some sales proposals and waited patiently for the chaos to begin.

At about 9:45a.m., he heard a shriek across the large room of cubicles. It was Martha, who had just been informed by Jim Sheridan that Jackson had been murdered in his apartment the night before. Martha never got upset and was always on an even keel, so when she screamed, several people stuck their heads up over their cubicle walls to see what the commotion was about. Zack did too, of course. He, along with a couple of others, raced over to see what was wrong. She was crying and her voice trembling.

"James was killed last night," she said in a confused, frightened tone.

"What??" shouted Lisa, while another colleague, Pete Marshall, stood there with his mouth wide open in sheer shock.

"You have got to be kidding me! I just cannot believe this shit," Zack said, feigning surprise better than most would be able to under the circumstances. "Martha, what happened, where was he??" Martha explained that Sheridan told her that Jackson was at home last night and attacked around 7:30.

She continued: "He was shot three or four times, I think, and Jim said he was cut into pieces! Oh my God, who could do something like this? He never did anything to anybody!" She started sobbing. Martha was 57 years old and the nicest person on Earth. Zack thought to himself that she was so sweet that she could overlook or possibly not even see the obvious faults of an asswipe like Jackson.

Pete looked down and around the floor, Lisa had gone back to her desk to probably call her hulking boyfriend, and everyone else had scattered around to start gossiping and reeling off a list of their own suspects. Zack stayed with Martha and comforted her. Sheridan had come down from upstairs to check in with the staff and give an impromptu speech on how big a tragedy it all was and how everyone would need to come together and try to move forward despite what had happened. About an hour later, the police arrived. Because it was such an elaborate killing, it was on the news, and reports stressed that Jackson was, of course, murdered but that there was no evidence that he had unlocked the door, so police were convinced it was someone he knew or someone who had a key, or both. They had questioned everyone else in the building and were now approaching his colleagues. When Zack saw detectives walk in to speak with Martha, he nearly vomited into his trashcan, but he kept his cool and about a half hour later, they arrived at his desk.

"Zack Williams?" posed one of the detectives. Zack nodded affirmatively. "I'm Detective Julian Wright and this is Detective Heather Pilson. We're from the NYPD and we'd like to ask you a few questions about Mr. James Jackson."

"Sure, go right ahead," Zack said, keeping his downcast look about him. "I don't know what to say, it's just mind boggling. You come in to work and never expect that you'll have a day like this."

"We know this is a difficult situation, and we appreciate you taking the time to talk to us for a few minutes," Pilson said, adding, "How long did you work for Mr. Jackson?"

Zack informed them that it had been just over a year and when asked by Pilson if the two had ever had any problems with each other, he was forthright. "We had our share of run-ins, typical sales manager to salesperson stuff," he said. "He didn't really like my work, to be honest. But he gave me the standard raise and he invited me to his home for a party once. We were supposed to meet this morning to revise a proposal I did for him the other day."

"Would you say that you liked Mr. Jackson?" Wright asked with a stone face.

"I respected Mr. Jackson, but I don't think I knew him well enough outside of the office to say that we liked each other or were friends," Zack said calmly. "I mean we didn't always argue, and we had several professional lunches together. He would even tell a good joke or two. He was just high strung, which in this business is commonplace. I just can't believe this shit." Zack teared up. Inside, he envisioned standing at a podium accepting an Oscar.

"A couple of your co-workers said they saw him yell at you on a few occasions," Pilson said.

"Yes, that's very true," Zack said, looking down. "I don't really think he liked me very much, if you really want to know, and I'm sure plenty of people will agree with you. But I relied a lot on his guidance and his contacts in the industry to help me, and this is a big void professionally for me and for this company. I know that the VPs really liked him because he was aggressive and got the most out of the staff, no matter what methods he might have used."

The detectives, especially Pilson, were clearly impressed with Zack's candid talk.

"Well, thank you for your time, Mr. Williams," Wright said, adding that if they need to speak to him again, they would give him a call or return to the office. Zack stood up to shake both officers' hands, and they walked off. As the detectives rounded a corner to speak with Pete, Pilson shot a serious glance back at Zack and immediately turned her head back to where she was going. Zack didn't know if she was flirting or if she secretly suspected him of something.

It turned out that several of Zack's coworkers vouched for him and told the detectives that Jackson verbally abused Zack a few times and that Zack was so sensitive that he would just sit despondent at his desk but never got angry or stormed out or anything. They thought he would be absolutely incapable of such a monstrous act against Jackson, or anyone else for that matter. Lisa had to answer more pointed questions about her boyfriend's epithet-laced tirade directed at Jackson after his sexist comments, but nothing came of it.

A week later, it was discovered that Randy, the mailroom guy, had actually threatened Jackson in public and threatened to hurt him in Times Square in front of at least 50 people, including Jackson's ex-wife and son, who were visiting at the time. Despite that being the only evidence of a problem between the two besides the office arguments they had, Randy was arrested for the crime and held without bail. He lost his mind when Pilson and Wright showed up to read him his rights, and backup officers had to pin him to the ground. When told of the arrest, Zack acted surprised but his coworkers didn't. They all agreed that Randy probably did it, and Zack shrugged his shoulders and went back to his desk. The department had been operating for a week without an associate publisher, and Sheridan informed the staff that, for the time being, it would stay that way.

Chapter 31

It was a glorious Christmas season in Montana, and Daniel Smith was preparing to do his annual civic duty. Each year, beginning December 1, he would dress up as Santa and go around Rossage and the surrounding towns giving away good cheer, and yuletide sweets, to kids and their families. Edmund would go along with him and, aptly, would be an elf. They enjoyed bringing a smile to the residents' faces this time of year. And they had reason to be so cheerful. The Everything Bar sales figures had come in from the test stores, and more than 60 percent of the candy had been sold in just a few months. That was an obscenely high number, and after Edmund made sure it was correct, the entire assembly line who worked on the bar was feted to a dinner at Sally's, the town's only luxury restaurant.

"I want to thank each and every one of you for making the Everything Bar a reality," Daniel said, holding up a glass of wine for a toast. "In just a few months, the sales figures were through the roof, and we're going to start mass production of the bars for New York, Los Angeles, and Miami starting next week!" Everyone at the table roared with applause. "I also want to take a bit of time and express my gratitude to your QCT, Greg Farber. His positive attitude and relationship with all of you made this possible. So let's also raise our glasses in honor of his efforts…thanks for everything, Greg." Everyone shared in a silent and solemn toast for Greg, having no idea that he could have cared less about any of them.

Chapter 32

Nothing is better than Christmas-time in New York City, Zack thought. Over the last couple of months, he had gotten past the Jackson episode and moved forward. Randy from the mailroom was scheduled for trial beginning in May and Zack had been able to control his impulses and anger. He was so frightened in October and November of being caught that he rarely left the apartment other than to go to work. He went out a few times in Queens but nobody else had seen him before the past Saturday, December 4. That day, he finally showed up at Maurice's for the Saturday afternoon drinkfest. The guys knew that his boss had been murdered, so they weren't too hard on him for not having come out much since, except for Puerto Rico Ron, who could have cared less if Zack's whole family had been wiped out. To Ron, there was no excuse for not imbibing with friends each and every chance one gets. It was a great time, and Zack felt like he was back to his old self.

He decided to make amends on this Monday for an appointment he missed several weeks ago, and that was to visit TapTown to see the beautiful Victoria Delgado. He left work and took the train ride uptown to 77th Street and walked over a few blocks and ventured inside. He didn't see Victoria. Maybe she was off today or changed her schedule, he thought. Zack was dejected, but he decided to have a beer or two, since he had gone so far uptown.

Zack sat at the bar and ordered a beer. The bartender, a tall and dark-haired man who was impossibly thin, was not the nicest in the city. Zack just stared at him as he poured the beer without saying a word. Zack already had a 10-dollar bill on the counter, so the bartender took it, put the change on the bar next to Zack, gave a thank you nod, and walked to the other end of the bar. He stood alone, peering out of the front window. Zack looked around and noticed that he was the only customer.

Thinking about his day, Zack sipped on the beer for a few minutes; then he heard footsteps coming up the stairs to the right of the bar. The steps got louder and then finally emerging was none other than Victoria Delgado. Zack's face lit up like a Christmas tree, and if he had meant for it not to, then he had done a horrible job of trying to hide it and play the part of a cool customer. The thin man left immediately, saying nothing. For Zack, after a two-month hiatus, seeing Victoria was like never having met her to begin with. She looked so stunning that he nearly spilled his beer all over himself. She walked into the bar area, put her things on the counter behind the register, and walked over. Stopping in front of Zack, she smiled and said, "Well, hello stranger. How have you been?"

"I've been horrible. My boss was murdered, and I was so busy after that and haven't had a chance to go out at all. In fact, this is my first time at happy hour in two months. But I am so glad I came."

"Me too," Victoria said, causing heart palpitations for Zack. "The last couple of months haven't been too much fun for me, and I hate working here, to be honest with you. But your boss! Murdered?? We can't talk about that today."

Victoria and Zack spent the next 30 minutes talking about everything else, from politics to relationships to work to family to alcohol. Finally, another customer came in. It was a random guy who, to no surprise, was also taken aback by Victoria's sex appeal. As she went to prepare a drink for the new customer, he looked at Zack and said, "Goddamn, have you ever seen anything like that behind a bar?" Zack replied with a laugh, "Nope, I can't say that I have." Victoria returned with the drink.

The man continued. "A woman with a body like that oughta not be allowed to work in public or around men at all." Before Zack, who normally would laugh but this time was furious, could even get a word out to tell this man to settle down, Victoria shot back.

"A man with a mouth like yours has never and will never see a woman with a body like mine without clothes unless he pays $3,000 for it upfront," she said with a blank expression, immediately walking away. Zack exploded in laughter. Unfortunately, so did the other patron, which made Zack look like he was siding with him at Victoria's expense. Zack quickly shut up, and the man, sensing Zack's loyalties, smirked at him, shook his head in disappointment, and went to play some pool on the other end of the bar. Zack immediately turned his attention back to Victoria.

"I'm sorry about that; I thought your statement was great."

"I know, that asshole laughed with you. I hate jerks like that. But I'm glad you liked my reply," she said with a more genuine smile. Zack had remembered the false grin from his moment smoking the cigarette with Victoria when they first met. Maybe he had made up for it this time.

"What do you say we go have dinner, you and me? I've got plenty of stories to tell and nobody to listen to them." Zack was desperate for her to say yes.

"That would be really cool. But it would have to be as friends. I'm going through a rough time right now."

Zack quickly agreed to the terms, knowing that it may be the biggest mistake of his life. "A rough time right now" never meant "just a bit later" in Zack's experience. Then he remembered that chopping up James Jackson and leaving his body parts around his apartment probably qualified as being a bit more of an error in judgment.

"OK, when do you want to get together?" Victoria said that Saturday would be a good night. She wrote down her cell phone number and email address on a napkin and handed it to Zack. Coming from the old school, Zack's work was done. Once he had a phone number, it was time to leave. So he bid Victoria adieu and nearly had a heart attack trying to walk coolly out of the bar. He smirked back at the random guy on his way out. He had a date coming up with the most beautiful woman he'd ever seen.

Chapter 33

Victoria told Zack she had never tried Armando's, a Mexican restaurant on 3rd Avenue in Manhattan that she heard was good. So the pair decided to see what all the fuss was about. They were to meet in front of the restaurant. Zack got there early and was holding up a sign, like a limo driver at an airport, which read "Delgado". Victoria was embarrassed when she walked up and saw it, but it amused her so much that she was nearly bowled over in laughter. Zack felt good. But neither of them felt good after the meal.

It was the worst Mexican food they both had ever had. They enjoyed the time they had there, however, mainly because they kept making fun of each dish that came out, one tasting as bad as or worse than the next. Although it was their first time out together, Zack got Victoria a small gift, since it was holiday time. It was, aptly titled, a gift card for her favorite lingerie store. Stunned, Victoria leaned over the table and planted a kiss on Zack's left cheek. He immediately said that there is no chance that he would ever willingly wash that spot again and that if it looked like he had, it would be because water just happened to go there during a shower or rainstorm. Again, Victoria was amused. She enjoyed Zack's jokes and sense of humor; and he enjoyed everything about her.

They decided to walk back to her place in East Harlem. It was about a 30-block walk, so they had ample time to talk. Victoria told Zack about her time in Florida, her sudden and courageous move back to New York, and her never-ending battle of wills against Frederico. Zack listened carefully, taking in every word she said. He was actually internalizing every word as if he and Victoria were married. He cared about everything she said, and even though he knew that he was going to get himself into trouble, he simply couldn't resist. He fell in love with Victoria after one date, a date that, to her, was one friendly date. No matter, Zack thought, he would do whatever it took to win her heart over. As it would turn out, 'whatever' would involve absolutely anything. They walked arm in arm for half the distance to her building. Victoria could quickly tell that she could trust Zack, and she had never trusted the right man in her life. He bid her goodbye at the front stoop of her building and watched her walk up the stairs. Then he resisted the urge to turn into Buzz and fly home in the cold, and he walked happily to the subway.

Chapter 34

"I like what you've done with the place, Zachary!"

And with that statement from Dorothy, Zack welcomed his parents to New York for the holidays. It was December 19, and Dorothy and Robert made it in from Texas without a hitch. If Dorothy said that Zack's apartment was nice, then Zack knew he was doing things right. His mother wasn't one to mince words when it came to cleanliness. Robert agreed but was mostly watching television and waiting to leave. He was hungry. So Zack got his coat and escorted his folks outside, hailed a cab, and went to Manhattan. His parents were staying in a hotel in midtown, since his apartment was too small. They checked in, and then they all went out for a steak dinner.

"Zack, I still can't believe your boss was killed like that," Dorothy said, prompting Robert to say, "Can we talk about something else right now? Jesus Christ." Zack's parents have always had humorous back and forth, although it is humorous mostly to everyone outside of the family.

"I can't believe it either, but everything is about back to normal now," Zack said.

"Did they catch the guy who did it?" asked Dorothy.

"Yeah, it's been on the news all the time," Robert retorted to Dorothy's rolling eyes.

The Williams family is a cross between the Cosbys and the Ewings: dysfunctionally functional. They are incredibly normal, yet there are times when not many people would be able to figure out just what is going on. Everyone in the family is very sharp and bright, and there is an enormous amount of love that each member has for the other. They laugh a lot, tell great stories, give out advice, and listen to one another. But each individual member has demons that shape who he and she are. However, it has become obvious over the last few months that the most dangerous of the family is Zack, despite his Victoria-infused calm demeanor lately.

The family finished dinner and everyone said goodbye to each other for the night. As Zack walked a few blocks to the subway, he wondered how disappointed his parents would be if they ever found out what he had done. He couldn't think about it for long because it made him sick. So he went home, keeping his mind on the good times he'd had with his family.

Chapter 35

Zack whistled his way out of the subway station in Queens. He had just spent some quality time with his family and had a gorgeous girl on his mind. He was about 50 feet from the front door to his apartment building. Going in ahead of him was a young woman, Antonia, who moved in a month ago on the same floor. She was nice to everyone but never said a word to Zack. Even the other residents on the floor noticed it. June, who is Zack's 80-year-old next door neighbor, mentioned it the other day in passing and said she would say something to Antonia if she didn't start being nicer to him. Zack laughed and gave June a hug, assuring her that it was OK and that she didn't need to confront her about it.

Zack walked through the first door of the building and was just about through the vestibule to the second door, which requires a key, when it slammed shut on him. Antonia decided not to hold the door for him. That would have been appropriate for her, Zack thought, seeing as though she didn't like him for some reason. But she paused while she was inside, turned around, gave a cruel glance to Zack, and kept walking. So he used his own key, walked in, and briskly strolled toward Antonia from behind.

"Hey, what was that about? If you have a problem with me, why don't you just say so?"

"If you keep harassing me, I am going to call the police. I know how you people are."

Zack froze in his tracks, and Antonia waltzed down the hallway, with a special spring in her step, and bounced into her apartment. Zack looked to the right. He was directly in front of his place. So he went inside, and put his keys down, stood for a moment looking down in front of his dresser, nodded his head in disappointment, and went about his business. He put his coat on the rack near the bathroom and went in to use the toilet.

Standing and watching the water cascade into the bowl, he glanced over to the right. The speed skating outfit was hanging off of the shower curtain rod. He stood there, staring at it for probably 20 seconds after he was done using the toilet. He zipped up, left the bathroom without flushing, and turned the television on. The story on the sports channel was about the lack of black coaches in college football. Zack got angrier and angrier as he kept thinking of how Antonia disrespected him. He tried to calm himself down, but he just couldn't. He decided to get some air. He grabbed his coat again and walked out. Antonia was standing at the mailbox checking her mail at the time. She rolled her eyes, turned and walked briskly back into her apartment, slamming her door and creating a loud echo.

Zack exhaled and walked out to the front of the building and walked down to the corner and then up the block. Looking left, he caught a glimpse of Antonia, whose apartment was on that side of the building. Her window was open. She was on the phone laughing. Zack went back to his apartment. He stormed into the bathroom and grabbed the outfit off the shower rod. He put it on and took along the surgical mask and gloves, but not the gun, and opened his window. He had forgotten the chant because it had been some time, so he grabbed the book out of his drawer and found it. He said the chant. Ready to roll, Buzz flew out and around the side of the building, resting on the open windowsill of Antonia Melotti.

Chapter 36

Buzz flew in and, as he did at James Jackson's place, rested on the couch of Antonia Melotti. She was thin, about 5-foot, 10-inches tall, and walking briskly around the apartment, smoking a cigarette and yapping on the phone with a friend. A copy of *Mein Kampf* and a hip-hop magazine were on her coffee table. Even with that, she befriended everyone on the floor except for him, he thought, shaking his fly head in disbelief. He was furious. He noticed a coupon for the tanning salon down the street from the apartment building as he flew over to the kitchen table. He overheard Antonia say "OK great, see you in a half hour. I'm gonna put on something more comfy." She hung up the phone and raced to the bathroom to shower. She left the bathroom door open.

Buzz rested on the kitchen floor and quietly chanted into a human. Zack stood up and turned the oven on to 700 degrees, left the oven door open, and reached up and disabled the smoke detector. He walked into the restroom and slowly approached the shower. Antonia was singing. He yanked the shower curtain back and Antonia turned, screaming for a half second before Zack grabbed her by the face, his entire palm covering it, and slammed her head into the shower wall, knocking her out cold. She fell to the basin of the tub. Zack dragged her out of the shower and back into the kitchen. To make sure she wouldn't wake up, he hit her in the head three times with the incredibly large *Mein Kampf* tome. He picked her up like a bride in colonial times, face down, and shoved her head first into the oven. Her head and shoulders fit in it and the rest of her body stuck out. Zack held her by her legs like a wheelbarrow in front of the oven as her head and shoulders cooked. After a few seconds, she woke up and began to wiggle and scream and fight to get out. But she didn't have enough strength and was finally dead. Zack held his ground and the wiggling stopped. He pulled her body away from the oven. Antonia's head hit the oven door after it came out and then hit the floor. Zack turned her body over. Her head was burnt to an absolute crisp and her eyes were red splotches, with only her teeth glistening among a black orb. Her hair was virtually burned off. He turned off the oven and got a knife from her kitchen drawer and cut open her stomach area. He couldn't believe what he was doing, but he felt a sense of calm amid the chaos. Reaching around inside of her body, he located her intestine, pulling it out enough to wrap it around the *Mein Kampf* and leave it tied to her body and leaning up against her hip. He took the tanning salon coupon and laid it across her now-lipless mouth and looked around. It was silent. Too quiet, Zack thought. He turned on her television, leaving blood on her remote control as he gently placed it on the coffee table next to the hip-hop magazine. He chanted. Then Buzz flew out the window and around the corner to his own apartment, turned into himself, hit the floor and looked up at the ceiling, his face awash with relief. Buzz and Zack were becoming quite intimate.

Chapter 37

Antonia's male friend showed up about 15 minutes after Zack got back to his apartment. Zack had been looking outside of his peephole and noticed a man walk by and up to her door. Getting no answer after several minutes, he walked back past Zack's door, presumably out of the building. Maybe he thought she ran to the store or was in the shower, Zack thought, an evil grin on his face as he walked to the refrigerator for some water.

A couple hours later, sirens blared in front of the building and two policemen raced to Antonia's door along with her friend. After yelling to find out if she was inside, the cops kicked the door in and everyone rushed inside. Zack could hear faint screams of "Oh my God!" and "Jesus Christ!" He sat back down on the couch and watched the sports news, knowing that a knock on the door was coming soon. He remembered to put his outfit and items under the sink. About a half hour later, the knock on the door arrived. Zack answered it but didn't open the door.

"Hello, sir, we are from the NYPD and would like to speak with you for a minute. Do you mind if we come in?"

"What's this about?"

"There's been a problem with one of your neighbors and we need to talk to the people on the floor please."

"OK," Zack responded, opening the door. Both policemen were clearly surprised, Zack could surmise, that he was black. Kew Gardens didn't have a lot of black residents. But, gathering their composure, they proceeded.

"Hello, sir. Sorry to bother you this evening. Do you know an Antonia Melotti? She lived down the hall from you?" The police didn't even introduce themselves in their apparent shock, Zack thought. The one who asked had a nametag that read Schultz.

"You mean the new girl? No, not really, she hadn't been here that long, I don't think. Why, is something wrong?" Zack looked down the hallway past the cops and saw a stretcher and some light smoke emerging from Antonia's apartment. "What the hell is going on over there?" The cops moved closer together and shielded Zack from seeing clearly. Zack could hear June sobbing next door while speaking to another officer. She suddenly yelled for Zack.

"Zack! Zack honey, are you over there? Something terrible has happened! Someone killed the new girl!" June was hysterical, and the cops allowed the neighbors to embrace in the corridor. The officers formally informed Zack that Antonia had been killed.

"By who? What the hell is going on?" Zack asked with an incredulous look. "I thought this was a secure building! Needless to say, I think, and June agrees with me I'm sure, that we need a little more security in this place!"

June certainly did agree, going on and on about how she had been in the building for 45 years and never did anything like this happen, and continuing on about how great her neighbors have been, especially Zack, and that Antonia was polite but never truly cordial to anyone. That got Zack's attention. He knew that Antonia was more than polite to everyone on the floor except for him. June was covering for him without even knowing that he did anything. It was an appreciated gesture, and Zack smiled warmly at June while all the cops were facing her and not him. She smiled in turn, and walked back into her apartment, still crying, as the police walked with her to make sure she was alright. Schultz asked Zack a few more questions that had little meaning, and then the two officers were off to file their reports. Zack went immediately to bed, letting well enough alone.

Chapter 38

At his desk the next morning, Zack had a soda and the morning paper. The headline inside read, *"Burnt to a Crisp – Queens woman massacred after one month in building."* Zack pressed his lips together, swallowed, and continued to read. Pete walked up.

"Man did you hear about that murder in Queens? It's in Kew Gardens," he shouted while whispering. "Don't you live in Kew Gardens? Man that is fucked up!" He immediately walked off. Zack sat there, frozen but calm.

He called his parents and set up a lunch with them downtown. He met them at a Thai restaurant near City Hall. He thought he could get through the entire hour without it coming up. But his parents had brought the paper with them. His mother began to read the story about the killing.

"Zachary! Isn't your address 709 75th Place? This happened in your building!" Dorothy said, staring intently at her son. Robert gave him the same look.

"Yeah, I didn't want to worry you both by telling you about it, but I guess you found out." Zack gave a nervous laugh. "She lived a few floors up though, so I only saw the cops go upstairs to check it out. It's not like I knew her or anything."

"Well, good," Dorothy said, absorbing Zack's lie, "Because I don't want them accusing you of anything. You know you would be the first person they'd go after." Robert nodded affirmatively, munching on some appetizers and not looking up. Zack turned the discussion to what they had been doing since they arrived, and the topic of murder didn't resurface.

Later that day, Zack tried to stop thinking about going up to TapTown but he couldn't do it. At 5:01 p.m., he was racing to the uptown train to visit Victoria.

Chapter 39

Victoria had taken Monday off. When Zack found out, he was devastated and sulked his way home. Victoria had gone on a trip with Frederico to the Catskills, in upstate New York. Unfortunately for Zack, the bar owner, Vincent, told him that. Zack gave Vincent a sarcastic look when he heard the news. He knew Vincent told him on purpose to make him mad; and he knew that when they were teenagers, Vince and Victoria had a relationship. It was a no-win situation for Zack.

All the way home, he was asking himself the usual questions a wanton man has for a woman he cannot have, like "What is it that she sees in these losers?" and "We're friends, and I've been polite and done things for her. Why won't she sleep with me?" But he knew the answers already. He was in denial about his role in Victoria's life. She liked him and thought he was friendly, funny, compassionate, decent looking, and a good man. But she didn't have thoughts of sexual attraction to him like he did to her. So he was completely out of luck. He knew that had he rejected her when she said she wanted to be friends that his life would be more uncluttered and he may have even ended up getting her because then she couldn't trap him with the friend tag when she knew damn well what his intentions were. All these thoughts weren't doing anything for Zack other than increasing his frustration level.

So he went home and ordered a pizza, eating the entire thing in less than an hour. Depression and food always went hand in hand for Zack, and tonight was no different. Thoughts of Victoria sleeping with Frederico, who she had shown him a photo of on their date, consumed him; he was losing it. He had run out of options, having broken off a short relationship several months ago and then not calling any of the women he knew during his time in hiding after the Jackson fiasco. Now he was alone, with no woman he could call on to take his mind off of Victoria. Not a good situation for Zack. He forced himself to sleep, making the mistake of playing some slow bebop-era jazz to help him drift off, thinking that by the time he woke up, it would all be better. But when he woke up, he felt just the same: angry and alone in New York.

Chapter 40

Frederico Salas has been in and out of the criminal justice system his whole life. A hustler, Salas has always been able to work his way through women and money. In the big city, being able to hustle, no matter your religion, race, or belief system, is the key to getting big money and big power. Salas knew how to do both. But, as is usually the case with the city hustler, the big money and big power are fleeting, and the normal result is jail or a hospital, or worse.

It was the hardscrabble projects of the South Bronx that forged Salas into who he was, a charming, strong, and street-smart smooth-talker, who was also known to the ladies as being well-endowed, which didn't hurt his reputation at all. Salas met Victoria years ago at a drug store. Victoria, who was 18 at the time, was getting something for her mother, and Salas was looking to steal some condoms, toothpaste, and deodorant. He was 10 years older than Victoria, which held appeal for her, like it does for many teenage girls. In short, Salas seduced her, and their affair would last until this day, when, lonely after deserting Martin in Florida, Victoria agreed to go to the Catskills with Salas.

She had sat night after night in her apartment, watching her phone ring and seeing through the caller ID that it was Salas. She even had other men over, and the phone would ring at least two times an hour. Finally, she relented and answered the call. Normally, the result would be an exciting time filled with danger and great sex. On this occasion, however, it turned out to be a mistake. Victoria was a lot older now and no longer interested in Salas' trash-talking ways and tough guy attitude. The fact that Salas had just finished a six-month stretch in prison for robbery didn't help either. But Salas was older then, and he was older now. He wasn't changing.

The clash occurred when Victoria, who just wanted someone to talk to and be close with who she was familiar with, resisted a sexual advance from Salas in their bed-and-breakfast room. Salas grew frustrated and grabbed her, his eyes wild with both anger and desire. Frightened, Victoria recoiled and ran out of the room and down to the front desk, threatening to call the police. Salas then immediately acted remorseful. He said to Victoria, in front of other guests and the older couple who owned the property, that the situation was just a misunderstanding. This forced Victoria to choose between calling the police in the Catskills (and starting a huge controversy in a town that didn't get many Latin visitors) or turning the other cheek to avoid an embarrassing situation. She relented but said nothing more to Salas for the remainder of that night and all the way home the next day. It was with that backdrop that she appeared with a long face on Wednesday at TapTown.

Zack walked in and an immediate smile came across her face. She felt she could trust him even more over the last few days and that she could tell him anything. Zack felt the same way, but he wanted a lot more than she was willing, or even wanted, to give. No matter. Zack was enthralled once again. But he sensed that something was bothering her the second he got to the bar. She took a break and told him what had happened, breaking down in the process. Zack had only known Victoria for a few months, but he was incensed at Salas and his blood was boiling. Victoria could tell he was upset and stopped talking about it for fear that he would do something stupid. But she was thankful that he was there to talk to. As he put his arm around her to comfort her, she opened up.

"Zack, you're such a real man. I haven't ever had a male friend that I could count on, who doesn't expect anything from me." Zack's head was above hers, so she couldn't see him roll his eyes with disappointment at her confirmation that he was clearly not a sexual interest. But he couldn't give up.

"I enjoy being there for you." Zack was dying inside to tell her his real feelings. "I can't believe that he would treat you like that after knowing you all these years. But it sounds like you two have always been lovers, so I guess there is an expectation that comes with that."

"You're right, Zack," she said, sniffing. "But I made it clear that I didn't want that to be a part of our relationship any more."

"But that may not be a realistic thing to imagine. The only thing you could do if you honestly want that to be the case would be to stop seeing him altogether."

Victoria agreed and, on top of that, she said it would be very simple. She would just tell him what the situation is going to be and let that be it. But Zack knew her well enough to know that she wouldn't be able to do that unless she had another lover already. Zack's curiosity had always gotten the best of him, even when he was a young boy. Now it would come back and get him again.

"So what's up this week, you got any plans?" he asked with an innocent look. Victoria said she had things to do until Saturday. Zack knew that she worked Friday night and Saturday during the day, so he thought she might have a date on Thursday. But he didn't say anything.

"Ok. Well, maybe we can get together soon and shoot pool or something."

Victoria agreed but was getting busy with customers and couldn't give Zack the acknowledgement he was looking for. So he waved to her while she worked and left to go home. On his train ride, he kept having thoughts he knew he shouldn't have and it was making him feel terrible and filled with guilt. In fact, ever since he had gotten back from Texas, things had been going in the wrong direction for Zack. He couldn't explain it at all. But the one thing he did know was that on Thursday, he was going to tell his parents that he had to work late and then use the chant for the first time in an effort to spy on someone; and that someone would be Victoria Delgado.

Chapter 41

Zack told his folks that he had to finish a big work project. Dorothy wanted him to go to the opera with them. Zack may have lied to get out of it even if he had no business with Victoria. He got home from work Thursday and had a quick TV dinner. He spoke on the phone with Cousin Benny and called Ron to find out what was up for Saturday. Then he kept his same clothes on, sans his tie, and changed to Buzz. He flew by train again over to Victoria's. He was a bit anxious when he got there, not just because he knew that what he was doing was wrong but also because for the first time he nearly got killed along the way.

Someone finally spotted him on the train and slowly rolled up a newspaper they were reading and took a swat at him. Fortunately, because Buzz is a special kind of insect, he flew away long before the swat came at him. But what if he wasn't paying attention? Everything would have been over. Or would he have turned back to Zack on the floor of the train car? He was thankful that nothing happened, but to whom? God certainly couldn't be in a very forgiving or saving mood, seeing as though Zack had slaughtered two people.

All's well that end's well, Zack justified, and waited at Victoria's building for someone to show up and let him in the front door. He didn't know which window to approach otherwise. After about 20 minutes resting on the stoop of her building, she appeared but not alone. She was already with someone. Buzz couldn't have been sadder than at the exact moment he saw her with the other man. But it wasn't Frederico, as Victoria said as they got to the stoop, "Thanks so much, Esteban, for dinner. It was really good. You want to come up for bit?" Esteban replied, "Yeah that would be great, but not for too long, I gotta get back home soon."

Buzz followed the couple up the stairway to Apartment L; L for Love, he thought angrily as he just flew in before Victoria closed the door behind her. But before Buzz could even rest on Victoria's countertop, she had thrown down her purse at the door, grabbed Esteban, and they began to go at it. Buzz was stunned. The pair was like wild animals, grunting and groaning, groping and grabbing at one another. They even looked a bit angry about it. Not as angry as Buzz or Zack or whoever he was or would ever be, he thought. They never moved from the spot just inside the doorway. Both naked in seconds, they dove to the floor on top of the pile of their own clothes and fucked like dogs. There was no way around it for Buzz, this was unemotional, cold, and raw sex at its finest. His fly eyes opened as wide as they possibly could when Esteban moved one way to reveal Victoria's heaving breasts. "My God, are you kidding me?" Buzz asked himself. If a fly could sweat, he was drowning.

Buzz went into a dream zone. All he could see was Victoria and nobody else, full lips pursed in passion, her jet black mane of hair flowing fully behind her, extending her aura by two feet, her marble-like eyes wide open and staring straight at the ceiling, her oversized breasts shaking with each Esteban thrust. His eyes followed the passion trail. Her hips were as smooth as silk and vibrating with a continuous, pulsating rhythm. She had a Brazilian wax. Buzz was simply amazed at how beautiful this woman was. Looking further down, however, reality snapped him out of dreamland. Esteban was drilling her, and Zack wasn't. Overcome by jealousy, sadness, and anger, Buzz flew out of the air conditioner vent on the other side of the room, unable to escape before Victoria screamed out her orgasmic spasms.

Buzz was in a daze flying over East Harlem. He didn't feel like taking the subway back home, so he decided to test himself and find out how far he could make it on his own. He wasn't tired at all. He was juiced up and angry after seeing what he didn't want to see but had to see, so he took a flyover down Park Avenue. As he ventured past 96th Street, he began to feel better about things, and by the time he was at 72nd, he realized that he was on direct approach to the MetLife Building above Grand Central Station. Zack was finally doing something positive with his new flying phenomenon, taking a tour of the city he loved. He looked to his left at the Chrysler Building. He was about 10 floors up, he imagined, since he was barely above most of the residential buildings in the 70s and 80s blocks. The office buildings began shortly thereafter, and he flew toward Vanderbilt Avenue and rested for a while on top of a car near an east side entrance of Grand Central. He didn't feel like going inside. It was cold and time to go home. He had a traumatizing yet exhilarating evening, and was ready to sleep it off. Buzz decided not take any chances going across the East River, and flew back up to 63rd Street and got the train home.

Buzz was resting on the train wall heading home, staring at two people wedged into a train seat. It was a black man and a white woman, but they didn't know each other.

The man, who was slim and looked to be in his early 40s, was obviously mad and uncomfortable with the woman being next to him, even though she was slim and making an effort to be accommodating. She wasn't touching him at all, but it was obvious that she was simply trying to keep a distance that would eliminate controversy. She wasn't leaning the other way out of contempt. No matter.

He kept elbowing the woman over and over. She tried to let it go and not pay attention, but after the sixth or seventh elbow to her side, she got up and stood across from the seat, saying "Jesus Christ, you gotta be fucking kidding me," as she rose from her seat.

The man looked at her with wild eyes and said "Fuck you, white bitch! This is my seat! Fuck that! I don't give a fuck about shit! Fuck it!" He looked around the entire train car at that point for a challenger. He looked crazy, plain and simple. A few people were staring at him, but most of the riders simply kept to themselves, as most New Yorkers do in these situations. Not Buzz.

Having been blessed with a solid upbringing, he couldn't believe this man had just treated this innocent person with this much disrespect. It was one thing to play the role of the hardcore New Yorker, Buzz thought, but to just be an asshole like that was unacceptable.

The woman began to cry and stormed out of the train at Kew Gardens. Buzz did not get off the train, as he should have. He stayed on the wall, staring at the mean man, who had fallen asleep. The man got off the train in Jamaica and Buzz followed him. The man even walked angrily, stomping to his apartment a few blocks from the station. His girlfriend or wife was in the kitchen when he went in and slammed the door, barely missing Buzz as he did so.

"Nigga where have you been?" The woman was screaming, telling the man that she had missed work because he was out with his friends spending their money on alcohol and dice games. A baby wailed in the background, but Buzz couldn't see it.

"Shut up, bitch, hell, I had shit to take care of." Buzz was incensed. Playing judge and jury in his mind, he decided that the situation was the man's fault and there would be no time for the man to tell his side of the story. The man went to the back bedroom and into the bathroom. Buzz followed him, quietly chanted into Zack in the bedroom, took off his belt and hid behind the bathroom door.

The man walked out and Zack wrapped his belt around the man's neck from behind, squeezing so hard that the man couldn't make a sound while being strangled. He kicked wildly and swung his arms back around trying to grab Zack's head, but Zack was much bigger than him and avoided any contact with him. The man nearly kicked his bedroom television off the table it was on. From the front of the apartment, Zack could hear the woman yelling "Get your ass up here and take care of your son for a change, motherfucker!" The man finally expired. Zack threw him on the bed, took the belt from around his neck, and put it back on his pants. He noticed a scratch on his arm. In a panic, he searched the man's fingers for which one had scratched him and found the digit that had blood and skin under the nail. He grabbed the scissors he saw on the dresser and snipped the top part of the man's right index finger off. Blood leaked slowly out onto the bed. The woman was on her way to the bedroom. Zack chanted and flew out of the room, passing the woman as Buzz just in time. As he flew around the apartment listening to her scream as she found her man dead on their bed, Buzz hovered over the baby, who was in a playpen in another room. The little boy was adorable, Buzz thought. He hoped the boy would grow up to live a better life; thinking maybe eliminating his sorry father would help. He flew out of the window and back to the subway.

When Buzz got back and changed to Zack, he took a shower and lay on the futon with no television, no lights, and no fan (Zack normally liked the sound of the fan to help him sleep at night). Complete silence was all he wanted. The man he killed was prejudiced and sexist. He knew that some would say racist, also, but Zack didn't think it possible that black people could be racist. Prejudiced, certainly, based on their experiences. But racist? Not in this country. Zack believed that every other race could certainly be racist, but black Americans, who were still thriving through slavery, Jim Crow, and laws that were amended but attitudes that weren't through this very day, could only be prejudiced toward those who were racist toward them. He remembered the time he told a white man at a bar that the difference between racism and prejudice was that racism is having no other reason for hatred other than the fact that someone's skin is different and that prejudice is bias against those who practice racism. The man walked off with nothing to say, as Zack recalled. But he let that discussion escape his mind now. His only thought was how to take Victoria away from all of her suitors. Zack drifted to sleep.

Chapter 42

Zack had a relaxing and wonderful Christmas season with his family and friends, which included spending an imbalanced amount of money on gifts for Victoria (which, of course, she loved). He saw his folks off at the airport. It was always a sad time for him. Unfortunately, they had to leave on the Sunday after Christmas this year because Dorothy had to work on Monday. Whether coming or going, he hated parting with them. He was able to get over it quicker because of Victoria. Zack got his best female friend a variety of different things, including gift certificates and a t-shirt with her lucky number on it. All of the items were based on things she had mentioned to him that she liked. She couldn't believe he had put that much thought into it, and she cried when she opened everything. Zack, sitting on her couch, was satisfied that it was a step in the right direction. But he kept glancing over at her front door.

"What is over there that you like so much?" Victoria asked, having no idea he was staring at the spot where she got laid recently. She then got a strange look on her face and changed the subject. Maybe she remembered that she got laid at the front door, after all, and thought the sequence was too weird to continue.

Zack refused to believe that Victoria might have thought he was ugly, which he thought was the real reason all women turned men away. Zack didn't believe, not for even a second, that any woman who said she wanted to be just friends with a man did it for any reason other than she thought the man was ugly. And he would argue the point if need be. Once, he told a woman who rejected him at a nightclub that if his name was Tom Cruise and he had a wallet full of cash, she would do things to him that God could never ignore on the day of judgment. She got up and started to walk away, but she never denied it, which indicated to Zack that he was right, even if there was an argument that he may not have been. If there was, she didn't use it. Regardless of that line of thinking, he managed to refuse to believe that it applied to Victoria. So he always tried to think of other reasons. His weight? He wasn't huge, but he wasn't thin either. His income? He made about $65,000 a year, not bad in some places, great in others. But in New York, it's a drop in the bucket to a hot woman, Zack thought. Forgetting about all of that, he just smiled as Victoria dove into her gifts, smiling so hard her gums were showing more than her teeth. He loved it, but it was bittersweet. Had he avoided the urge to spy on her, he wouldn't have the flashbacks, so he swallowed his pride and tried to move on from it.

Zack had to endure an excruciating New Year's Eve alone in his apartment. Victoria had plans, and Zack didn't want to spend it with anyone else and spend a lot of money for nothing. So he struggled with himself and watched TV, counted the ball drop with his parents over the phone, called and left Victoria a Happy New Year message, and then went to sleep at 12:06 a.m. A few weeks later, Zack finally got a chance to get back to one of his old pastimes: partying. The Super Bowl had arrived. One of Zack's favorite days, Super Bowl Sunday this year featured Tennessee and St. Louis. That was good for Zack. He didn't care about either team, so he could concentrate on eating snacks and partying the day away. He met the guys at Maurice's. They had a good time, got some free promotional stuff, like keychains, and the game was great. But it was late when the game ended. Having had a bit to drink, Zack didn't feel like waiting for the train, so he decided to hail a cab.

He said his goodbyes, left the bar, and walked down to the corner. He extended his left arm into the street and watched as available cab after available cab whizzed past him. This was nothing new, but it never failed to incense Zack. A drunken white couple staggered out of a bar near the corner where he was standing, 73rd and 2nd Avenue, walked 20 feet further down the street from Zack, and a cab stopped almost immediately and scooped them up. Zack's anger had reached the boiling point. It had been so long, but that was it. He no longer could take it. He walked halfway down the next block and stood in the middle of it. The street direction was headed downtown, to his left. He waited to hail a cab until the streetlight to his left reached yellow. He saw the yellow light arrive, stuck his arm out, and sure enough an available cab passed him again but was stopped at the red light. Zack knew the cabbie would look in his side view mirror to see if Zack was staring at him. So Zack looked the other way for a few seconds, then ran top speed to the back, left-side door of the cab and jumped in while it was at the red light. Zack immediately started screaming.

"Why didn't you pick me up? You know it's illegal not to pick up a fare!"

"I am off duty!" the cabbie screamed in a foreign accent. "I am off duty, get out!" Zack wasn't going anywhere.

"I am calling the police right now, motherfucker, right now!"

"OK, OK, I take you where you want to go, goddammit!"

"It shouldn't be a burden on you, motherfucker! Your light was on, so you were available. Hell, now I don't even trust you to take me where I wanna go! Take me to 168th and St. Nick."

The driver, who had a foreign accent, was furious and screaming at Zack, who stayed quiet and let him stew for a few seconds. He knew that cabbies don't pick up blacks that often because they don't want to drive way uptown, a stupid line of thinking, Zack thought, seeing as though the fare is more money for them. Of course, to Zack the main reason was because they believed the stereotype that a black man would have a greater chance of robbing and killing them, stealing their cab, and driving to God knows where;

Zack thought to himself that if they continue to pass blacks by, they ought to expect to be robbed and beaten, and the way to correct it is pretty logical. Pick up black fares.

Zack looked at the nameplate on the back window. The man's name was Aziz. Zack leaned forward and calmly said, "Oh, I forgot, Aziz, I have to make another stop. Take me to 17th Street between 1st and 2nd avenue, thanks." The cabbie said nothing and changed direction when he could.

The cab rolled slowly down 17th Street between 1st and 2nd Avenues, a very quiet area, about 10 minutes later.

"Stop right here," Zack said about halfway down the block. "You oughta take five dollars off the fare for trying to pass me."

"Ten-sixty is the total," the cabbie said, facing forward and holding his hand out. Zack reached into his pocket and pulled out the keychain he got at Maurice's. It had a sharp-edged bottle opener on the end of it. He gave the cabbie a 10-dollar bill with his left hand. The cabbie said "Where is the rest of it?" Zack said, "Right here, hold on." He then reached up with his right hand and quickly went past the cabbie's head, digging deeply into his skin and slicing his neck back toward himself with the jagged edge of the bottle opener, opening the cabbie's throat.

The cabbie coughed and gagged and blood rushed out of his neck like a waterfall down into his lap and all over the steering wheel and dashboard. His body jerked all over the driver's seat side. Zack threw some loose change at him and punched him in the side of his head, saying "That's for all the black people you left on the fucking street, you son of a bitch." He got out and walked down a few feet, said the chant, and flew off. His adrenaline was high, so he flew straight out over the East River and north into Queens and found his way home. He put the keychain in the trash chute. Monday was garbage day, and his latest weapon would be gone forever before noon.

At the office on Monday, Zack had his newspaper. This time, the front page read "FARE CUTTER." Underneath, it read *"Hardworking cabbie's throat sliced near East Village."* Zack thought to himself, "Hardworking my ass. If I could have nailed all 15 cabbies who passed me, I would have, and this would be a hell of a news day! And I paid that fucking fare too!" His attitude was souring. His thoughts were suggesting that he accepted his actions and was less and less upset about committing these heinous crimes. He had killed four people. He had ended their lives. They had families, people who loved them. But he thought they didn't love their fellow man enough to continue living, and he felt justified in his actions. For Zack, it wasn't enough to care about one's family and close friends, a true man of substance made an effort to treat people he didn't know as if he knew them. Zack felt like he did that, so why couldn't everyone else? Not many people at the office discussed the cabbie story. Zack, further distancing himself from the situation, thought it was because the victim was an Arab.

Chapter 43

Two months passed by in the blink of an eye. Zack began to feel withdrawn. He remained on an even keel at work, and his relationship with his coworkers was as good as it ever was. But he looked more and more despondent when he was out, and his friends never truly asked what was wrong with him. He was emailing and communicating with his new best friend, Victoria, nearly every day, but had grown accustomed and somewhat weary of her stories about other men in her life and yet how wonderful he was. If he was so wonderful, why hadn't they made love yet? He didn't feel like talking to her for a while. Besides, only Puerto Rico Ron seemed to really notice how bad it was getting.

"Yo, Z-man, let me ask you something," Ron said on a lonely Wednesday night at Maurice's. "You've been looking like shit the last few months, ain't saying nothing to nobody. I know you want that Vulcana or whatever her name is, I forget, but what's really going on with you?" Zack roared back in laughter. Only Ron could joke like that about Victoria and make Zack see his own obsession in a humorous light. He told Ron that he had been working too hard since his boss was killed and that the company refuses to replace him so the staff is hard-pressed, and he said that he'd been lazy lately. "Motherfucker please, you need some pussy," Ron said, laughing hard afterward. "You better go on and call up that freak you brought by here that one time."

Ron was referring to Yvette, a Haitian lady Zack had seen for a few months in early 1999. Zack had dumped her because he found out she worked for the government and had spied on his personal records. She was a great lay though, and he could probably have gotten her to come over and screw him if he called, since she felt an enormous amount of guilt for pulling his file behind his back. She also identified with Zack on lots of levels because, being black, she understood all of the inner turmoil that can affect people on their side of the fence. Dorothy loved her; and Dorothy didn't like many women in Zack's life. She was tough on them. But Dorothy, Zack recalled, always scratched the surface, without going any deeper. Zack knew that if he saw Yvette again, he might get angry about the whole episode and kill her. Giggling to himself, Zack told Ron he was right and, tired of talking, told Ron he was heading home. But he wasn't heading home. For the first time, Zack wanted to drink alone.

He took the train downtown to a remote bar he had noticed one day near Wall Street. He walked in, and nobody was there. Perfect, Zack thought. It was a small pub called the Irish Beacon. Zack had a glass of scotch and sat on a stool in the corner of the bar, leaning up against the wall and having half his view obstructed by a video game system anchored to the bar. He was content to go over his thoughts and sip liquor. It was just 7:30 p.m., plenty of time to get home and relax. Without warning, the doors to the bar opened like a saloon, and about 25 cops, some in uniform, some plainclothes, barreled in and sat everywhere. Obviously, they were now off duty. Or were they, Zack wondered. He had seen a few stories about on-duty cops getting trashed and then plowing into families on the street over the years.

"Hey buddy, what's happening?" asked one cop very loudly. Zack answered, "Not too much, how's it going?" The conversation ended there. Zack didn't get along too well with cops. He had seen a friend of his in Texas get beaten by two cops who wrongly accused the pal of accosting a woman. When Zack tried to intervene, he got a billy club to the ribs. Six years later, and it still hurt from time to time on the left side of his chest. The seat next to him at the bar remained free for a half hour. Zack was playing a video game and sipping his second glass of scotch when someone finally sat in the seat next to him and said hello. It was a female voice, firm and commanding but soothing at the same time. Zack took his eyes off the video game for a second, glanced to his right, and said "Well, what do you know? Detective Pilson, right?"

Chapter 44

Heather Pilson grew up in Brooklyn, the daughter of a cop, the sister of two other cops, and the granddaughter of another cop. She still lived in Brooklyn, in Williamsburg. Needless to say, when it became apparent that she was a tom-boy, she was encouraged to follow in the family footsteps. But Heather didn't really want that life. It was forced on her by family peer pressure. She told Zack as much as they sat at the bar, playing video games between statements and absorbing the curious and not-so-friendly eyes of the other couple dozen police officers scouring the pub. Every few minutes, a different cop would come over and feel her up or say hello, just to interrupt the conversation. Zack loved it. His skin was his sin, and he loved to be a sinner.

"That's what I mean," Heather said. "You get a lot of those looks when you hang out with someone who isn't a cop, especially someone who is black and isn't a cop." Heather was a tall and slim woman, with All-American looks, wavy blonde hair, blue eyes, and a girl next door smile. She was very attractive in some ways, and extraordinarily ordinary in others. Zack didn't care. He was too busy playing video games and getting drunk off scotch to notice. To him, Heather was a cop, with a whole lot of other cops staring at her, drawing attention to him when he was just trying to drink alone. To Zack, there was no way that at least 10 of the other cops in the bar weren't simultaneously calling her a "nigger lover." But he never told her to go away. They had an interesting talk. Zack always liked to get perspectives from females. He usually was trying to figure out if they were lying or not, and he would often challenge them on anything he heard that he thought may not be true. But he let Heather say whatever she wanted. Maybe it was because nearly all of the bar patrons had a Glock and a billy club. She mentioned that Randy, the mailroom attendant who was arrested for the Jackson murder, pleaded guilty to 2nd degree manslaughter and took 10 years in prison. Zack was dumbfounded. He then mentioned that he took note of her intense glare at him when she and Detective Wright had come to see him at his office after the Jackson murder. Heather said that was because she wanted to see if Zack was affected by Wright's line of questioning, which can be considered harsh when taken along with his trademark scowl, she added. She also volunteered that she wanted to look back, just because. Zack had a warm smile and said he appreciated the compliment and that he needed it. Heather said she needed to give one out, because it had been a while since she had. Zack sensed that he needed to leave, as the stares grew even stronger from the other cops; so he closed his bar tab and paid cash, lest the bartender get his credit card information and address and gleefully pass the information around the room of policemen.

"Well, Heather, I better be on my way."

"I understand, probably a good idea. I'm heading home myself soon. I'm sure I'll see you again, now that I know where to find you for questioning."

"I don't really like this bar, but I'm sure you could figure out other places to find me if you really tried." Zack followed his flirty reply by getting up to leave. Heather had a wry smile as Zack descended from the stool to the floor and navigated through the maze of cops near the door, looking straight ahead. Only one cop said anything to him: "You aren't leaving yet, are you? The party's just getting started. Say it ain't so!" Zack kept going and took the subway home.

Zack took a long shower and was in a good mood. Scotch always put Zack in a good mood. He even cleaned up his place a bit, putting some papers and clothes away. He moved his gun and put it in the cabinet behind some paper plates. He was watching sports highlights and had turned the lights off when the front door buzzer went off. At 11 p.m., Zack was very wary of whom it could be, but normally at this hour it was someone who forgot their key. Zack didn't care, so he buzzed the person in and looked out of the peephole to see who it was. A shadowy figure in a long coat and skullcap was walking toward the door. Zack had no idea who it was but thought he must have the wrong apartment. So when the person knocked, Zack quickly answered the door and was prepared to tell the man he had the wrong place when he noticed that it wasn't a man at all. It was Heather Pilson.

She pushed Zack back into the doorway, closed the door behind her, took off her skullcap and shook her hair out, and without a word starting kissing him. Not believing what was happening, Zack kissed back but his eyes were wide open. He reached behind her and locked the door while she unhooked her coat to reveal only lingerie. Zack thought to himself that this only happened in the movies and that he was sure it was a setup and some cops were going to barrel the door down and kill him, accusing him of sexual assault. But it was no frame job. Heather kissed him so passionately that he gave in and they guided each other to the futon and fell on it. Heather did everything one could imagine a man would want in the hour-long sex session they shared. Zack, who returned all of Heather's favors and then some, thought to himself during the episode that she must have walked in on her brothers watching porn flicks many a time to have mastered the things she was good at, which was pretty much every specialty sex act in the book, as well as the ones that went unpublished. It was intense, and then it was over.

"My God, I wanted you," Heather said, her first words since arriving.

"I take it you had my address from the visit you and Wright paid me at work. I gotta tell ya, Heather. This was absolutely the biggest surprise I've ever had from a woman, and I am damn happy about it." He invited Heather to borrow a t-shirt from the dresser drawer to relax her lithe body in. She chose a long black t-shirt with no sleeves that stopped just above the bottom of her hips.

"I knew you'd appreciate it," she said, resting her head on Zack's chest. "Thank God my next shift isn't until tomorrow night." Taking his cue, Zack reached over, grabbed his cell phone, and left Martha a message. He wasn't going to be at work tomorrow.

Chapter 45

Heather left around 3p.m. that Thursday afternoon. She and Zack were very compatible in bed and got along well out of it also. She told Zack that she was usually off on Wednesdays and Sundays and that she'd love to come back but would understand if she weren't invited, due to her coworkers not really taking to him at the bar. Zack said not to worry; he would call at some point. She had a slightly melancholy look as she left. Zack let her go, unsure of what to say to her. He had been as reassuring as he was going to be on this day.

Zack made himself a sandwich and turned on the TV to watch a movie. Taking a drink of water, his phone rang. It was Victoria. She never called during the day. Zack answered it, of course.

"Zack! Zack! Are you there?" Victoria shouted.

"Yeah babe, it's me, what's going on?"

"He said he'd kill me! He shoved me and then he threatened me! I cannot believe it, after all I've done for him! That bastard!" She broke down in tears.

"I'll be right there."

Zack hung up immediately. It took him exactly six minutes to get in the shower to wash Heather off of him, put on some fresh clothes, brush his teeth, and be out the door. Forty-five minutes later, he arrived at Victoria's, out of breath. She had calmed down considerably since the phone call and gave Zack a hug and told him to sit on the couch. Zack had wanted her to still be hysterical so he could play the hero, but it wasn't to be.

"You want something to drink, baby?" Victoria asked. Zack nodded. She brought him some water and sat down next to him. "I don't know what to do, Zack. Frederico found out I was seeing Esteban from time to time and went wild, like we're married or something. If he knew I had gone out on a couple other dates he would've been even worse."

"What other dates?" Victoria knew why he asked the question. She knew he was in love with her, and Zack knew that she knew. So there wasn't any awkwardness. They both knew the situation.

"I've seen a few guys since I came back. I was lonely and just wanted some companionship. Now everyone thinks I belong to them. And trust me, Zack, I belong to nobody." Zack's entire body was smiling, but his face still looked sincere.

"Look, I'm sure Frederico was just frustrated because he has known you the longest and doesn't want to let go," Zack said in a fatherly manner. " Just let him cool down, and in a week or so, he will be over it and you can tell him at some point that you've moved on from where you were with him before you left and it's time for him to do the same."

"Zack, why are you so good to me? I'm not that great a girl."

"I don't know," Zack said to a surprised look from Victoria. "Lots of things, I guess. Or it could be that great things come in confusing, strange, convoluted, beautiful packages." Victoria laughed gently and held on tight to Zack's arm, a tear rolling off her cheek down onto his hand that was resting on her thigh. Victoria didn't deserve this treatment, he thought, vowing to wait a week to let the dust settle before he took care of the problem on his own.

Chapter 46

Frederico was on the Grand Concourse in the South Bronx doing what he does best, hustling. After a couple of hours saying hello to a few friends on the block, making some calls, and setting things up with a few ladies for later that evening, he decided that this Saturday afternoon was over.

Heading up to his apartment a few blocks away, Frederico told himself that whatever he did, he had to stay away from the cops. He was on parole, and even the slightest bit of trouble coming his way would end up sending him back to prison. He went to the couch, turned on the stereo, and began lifting a few dumbbells to the beat. On the arm of the couch on the other side of him sat Buzz, who had come over a couple hours prior to survey his place. Zack had looked up the address from a story about the robbery Frederico was involved in that he found at the library. He then saw the apartment number on the wall of the building.

Frederico was a strong man, Buzz knew, so he needed to plan this venture so that he didn't end up dead. But as it turned out, Frederico made it easier for him by enjoying something many men don't partake in too often as they get older: a bath. Buzz had noticed the bubble bath liquid on the side of the tub when he was flying around earlier and figured that if Frederico exerted any energy today he would probably take a bubble bath instead of a shower. Buzz was right.

Frederico dropped the dumbbells and walked to the bathroom, took off his clothes, and started to run the bath water. He put his gun on the ledge in the tub while the water was running. Buzz did his chant during this time also, so that he could find somewhere to hide while the noise he made was covered by the running water. Just as Zack slipped into a closet, the water stopped. Zack had forgotten his gun, so he needed to be smart. He had noticed earlier that Frederico kept a hair dryer plugged in on the sink next to the tub. Fortunately for Zack, Frederico had also pulled the shower curtain closed, even though he wasn't showering, and had turned on some music on a small stereo near the door. Zack tiptoed as silently as possible through the bathroom entrance, and picked up the hair dryer. In one motion, he turned it on, pulled the curtain, and threw it in the tub. A stunned Frederico managed to squeeze off one shot from his gun that whizzed past Zack, just past his ear, and into the mirror above the sink. Frederico was strong and resilient, but he fried for about 10 seconds before finally succumbing to the electrocution.

Zack immediately drained the water from the tub and pulled out the hair dryer by the cord. Frederico's eyes were wide open and his face had an angry and shocked expression, simultaneously. It was frightening. But not as frightening as what sat between his legs. Zack stopped for a second and had a confused look. The reputation was accurate. Frederico was hung like a bull. He was so endowed that it wasn't worth being jealous about. He had it like that, and that was it. But not any more, Zack thought. He left him in the tub and walked back to the living room area. He knew Frederico was connected to some gang activity in the area and had also read that gang members often liked symbolism in their killings. So did Zack. He took the dumbbell and held it by one end, slamming the other end into Frederico's dead face until he had hacked away his entire mouth, leaving nothing but dangling flesh from the nose on down, straight through to where the top of his spine was visible. He left the teeth and gums and lip and jaw bones and flesh scattered around the tub and stuck to the dumbbell, which he placed across Frederico's thighs. He then draped Frederico's huge penis over the dumbbell bar. Somehow, Zack had respected the endowed victim enough to let his dick go out with dignity. He then took Frederico's own gun and shot once into each eye, obliterating the sockets and leaving the gun on his chest. Neighbors were trying to beat the door down, and the bathroom window couldn't be opened. So Zack chanted and morphed into Buzz, and flew high near the ceilings as the neighbors burst into the apartment, looking around, until one started to scream upon finding Frederico. Satisfied, he flew out of the apartment, made a quick aerial view of Yankee Stadium, and took a leisurely flight home.

Victoria relied on Zack for moral support for the next month. She was really hurt by Frederico's death, even though she understood that it was entirely possible that he would be killed in a gruesome manner because of his lifestyle. She needed to get away from it all, so she and her friend Juanita went for a two-week vacation in the Caribbean.

Chapter 47

Zack's life was a bit better by June. But Victoria was going to the Caribbean too often for his tastes. She had just called him from there, her third trip there in a month and a half. Ridiculous, Zack thought. He knew something was going on. And he was right. Victoria returned to New York on June 13. She was excited to see Zack, but he wasn't as excited to see her. He was smart enough to know that what she was happy about would not make him happy. Sure enough, she ran up to him at TapTown with an engagement ring on her finger.

Zack congratulated Victoria and gave her a hug and then said he felt queasy. He left one minute later without saying a real goodbye, which to Victoria meant a hug and a kiss. But Zack didn't want to be near her, and she knew it. And she knew why. Zack thought that for her to even think he would be truly pleased for her was incredibly ridiculous. Zack had never been that hurt. He went in the bathroom on the way out, walked into the toilet stall, closed the door, and cried his eyes out, balling his fists in anger and heartbreak. He had to stop when another man walked in. He dried his eyes and left, looking down.

He went down to the Irish Beacon and played video games. Nobody was there, so he and the bartender, who was friendlier with no cops around, talked about sports and how horrible women were. Obviously, both of them had been recently spurned. The bar began to get crowded, and Zack overheard four drunken white women talking about men.

"I would have to be absolutely smashed to fuck a black guy," one of the women said. Zack laughed to himself and kept playing his video game. They had no idea he was close enough to hear them, nor did they notice he was even there. He could see who said it by her reflection in the video screen.

"Yeah, I hear ya sister," said another one. "Now, Denzel? No alcohol required." They all laughed hysterically.

"You know what we should do," the third one said. "We should do an advertisement thing, where we get a cute black guy to come over for a special party and get bombed and then just screw the shit out of him. God, would that be great or what? Our so-called boyfriends would never have to fucking know about it. They're racist anyways." Like they weren't, Zack thought. They all liked the idea so much that they actually decided to do it. By then, Zack was so mad at them that he decided to show them all what they were missing.

He immediately left without drawing attention to himself and walked across the street to a dark space between two buildings and waited and waited. Finally, the ringleader, the woman who sparked the idea, walked out of the bar, trashed and humming to herself. Zack morphed into Buzz and followed her inside the cab she hailed to Tribeca. In her apartment, he could see a piece of her mail. Her name was Annie Golden. She got a drink of water, shed her clothes in the bedroom, used the restroom, and got out a pad and pen. Buzz hovered above her as she wrote down what she would submit for the ad. It was to be published in an alternative magazine, the *Fetish Journal*. She went to her computer and entered the ad online at the publication's website. Buzz could see that it was to be published and available starting at 7 a.m. the next day. He then left, and flew top speed to his apartment to get some rest so he could be clear-headed enough to be the first to answer the ad.

By 6:45 the next morning, Zack, still torn up inside over Victoria, had arrived at an all-night Internet café all the way in the Bronx. He looked up the ad. It wasn't posted yet. At 6:48, he checked again. It was there. He immediately responded with: "Hello there. I noticed your posting seeking a black male to spend time with four professional, downtown ladies. I believe that I would qualify for what you seek. I am 5-foot, 10-inches tall, weigh about 185 (he was lying by about 20 pounds), and work out regularly. I am also a professional who works in midtown for a financial services company and I am experienced in non-work-related activities. I would love to hear from you. Please contact me via email and then we can talk. For safety purposes, I don't give out my real number and will call you back from a pay phone. But my name is Tyrone. I look forward to speaking with you." He gave her a new email address that he had made up. He used Tyrone as his name, because it was the most stereotypical name he could think of and would leave no doubt to the foursome that he was black.

He hoped that it was enough. Zack knew he was the first to contact Annie and that if he could talk to her for a few minutes, he would be chosen. He didn't want to use his work computer for any correspondence. So he left the office at 5 and went to a different Internet café in midtown to check the messages. Annie had written back and left a phone number. He traveled to a pay phone in Brooklyn to call her back. Zack used his extremely professional phone voice with Annie, putting her at ease. He asked if she was certain that this was something she and her friends wanted to do. Annie was emphatic with her affirmation. They loosened up and had a conversation that was much more relaxed after the first few minutes.

Annie worked for a Fortune 500 company, as did her cohorts. They were all attached but unsatisfied and tired of being bossed around by men who didn't satisfy them or do anything they wanted, she said, and they were tired of standing around with their men while they told crass jokes, talked about sports, and made racist remarks all the time. They were fed up and wanted a release. Zack played along and Annie gave him her Tribeca address. They settled on Sunday afternoon at 3p.m., right in the middle of their boyfriends' golf get-together. Annie said that to help relax the mode, they would all need a good amount of alcohol. Zack, who already knew that the real reason they wanted to drink was because it would lessen their inhibitions and put their racist tendencies on the shelf, said cheerfully that he would bring the beer and not to worry. Annie was excited, and hung up saying she looked forward to meeting. The foursome spent the rest of the week on Cloud Nine, secretly knowing that they were going to fulfill their collective fantasy: screwing a man they felt was inferior to them to get back at their lame boyfriends and fulfill their secret taboo desires.

Chapter 48

Sunday arrived. Zack woke up and went over to the diner for breakfast and to read the paper. He went home and watched some television, called his parents, and spoke to Cousin Benny for a few minutes. It was noon. He then put on his outfit, secured his materials, and chanted. Buzz flew over Queens and into Manhattan, over to Hell's Kitchen, and found a remote alley. He converted to Zack again, approaching a sleeping homeless man with a fifty dollar bill.

"Hey bud, what's up?" Zack asked as he approached the man, crouched in an alley with a dirty blanket on some cardboard. If you get me a mini keg of Smitty's and two 32-ouncers of whatever you want, I'll give you 50 bucks and have a drink with you when you get back." More than happy to oblige, the man rose up and asked for the money first. Zack gave it to him, stood in the alley, and waited. He decided to hide behind a dumpster in case cops happened to walk by and see a black man in a speed skating outfit in the alley. Everything went smoothly, though.

The man returned with a mini-keg of Smitty's, as asked for, and two other beers. He and Zack polished them off, talking for a while about how life can be a bitch. Zack bid the man adieu and took the mini keg further back into the alley as the man watched. Zack then chanted and disappeared. The homeless man rubbed his eyes in disbelief, shrugged his shoulders, and went back to sleep.

Buzz, armed with the mini-keg of Smitty's and his regular materials, traveled through the summer sky above New York, leisurely floating over to Annie's place. He wondered how in the hell the mini-keg could reduce in size like he could. But it was too much to think about. At around 2:50 p.m. he flew into Annie's building past the doorman and up to her floor. Someone was walking toward the elevator, so he rested on a wall until he was confident that he would be alone. He flew down to the floor, whispered his chant, and was in front of Annie's door with the mini-keg. Annie answered. She had just gotten out of the shower and looked pleasantly surprised. She was moderately overweight but well refined and very clean, Zack noticed. Her nails were perfect and she was plain but attractive enough. He shook her hand and walked in. The three others were in the living room already, watching television and looking quite timid when Zack walked in the room. But Zack was a salesman, so he put everyone at ease with a broad smile and some light, joking banter. The other ladies, introduced as Jamie, Amy, and Katherine, were similar in build and appearance. Zack thought to himself that Jamie was cute and skinny, Amy was bland but a thick body type, which Zack liked, and Katherine was mean looking. It really didn't make a difference to him, one way or the other. He sat down and Annie brought some cups in. They were going to start having that party. They all relaxed. Annie apologized for not having any wine or other alcohol. Zack didn't mind at all, and all of the ladies enjoyed the Smitty's. They had never heard of it, and Zack said it was an import from Ireland that was rarely sold in the USA but that if they looked hard enough, they could find it.

An hour later, all four of the ladies were drunk. They were telling jokes and touching Zack and touching each other. Zack was laughing and hamming it up, enjoying the moment. He was with four drunken women specifically getting liquored up to have sex with him; except everyone was drinking Smitty's. It seems that only Zack knew that Smitty's was nonalcoholic beer. Zack thought to himself, "How dare these people try to fool a fetish-monger like me?" Laughing inside while incredibly mad, and the confirmation of their racist and deceptive ways accomplished, Zack was prepared for the final act of this drama.

The women, who continued to act as drunk as the homeless man Zack dealt with earlier, asked Zack to do a strip tease for them. "Come on, Tyrone, you know you wanna hit this fat ass," a pseudo-drunk Amy said seductively, rubbing her butt against Zack's knee. He got up in the center of the room and the ladies surrounded him, dancing. Each woman got on her knees and kissed and licked his genitals through the speed skating outfit as he slowly twirled to a music video on the TV. "What's next, Mandingo?" Jamie asked. Zack was at the pinnacle of anger, yet excited by the attention. What man with a pulse wouldn't be, he thought. But he had to stay focused.

Zack stepped away from the group, turned his back in step to the rhythm, put on his gloves and surgical mask as the excited ladies wondered what skit was about to happen, pulled out the gun, turned around, and shot each of them once in the forehead. They were so stunned after the first shot entered Annie's skull that only one of them, Katherine, could even muster a scream. They were all dead, with the last four bullets Zack had left, within eight seconds. Knowing someone would hear the shots, he quickly took everyone's clothes off and balled them up together and put them in a pile to the side. He ran to the kitchen and got a long cake-cutting knife.

He arranged the ladies side by side on the living room floor, and struggled to cut each one's head off. He then put a different head on each body and opened all the eyes. He then cut off each of their breasts and rearranged them, placing Jamie's breasts on Annie's body, Katherine's breasts on Amy's body, Amy's breasts on Jamie's body, and Annie's breasts on Katherine's body. There was so much blood everywhere that Zack slipped and fell in it, hitting his knee hard on the floor. He picked up the mini-keg, picked up his cup of beer with his saliva on it, chanted, and flew out of an open window he found in Annie's bedroom. Arriving home, Zack showered and sat on the edge of the futon, looking down. He burst into a tear-filled rage, screaming with agony and crying so hard that it gave him multiple head rushes. He had now killed nine people and was getting angrier and more aggressive every day. He didn't know, nor did he care, how he was pushed over the edge. All he knew was that anybody who triggered his anger was going to die a miserable death, that he couldn't control it, and that it made him incredibly happy and extremely unhappy at the same time. It was an abstract feeling, and Zack never dealt with abstracts. He was living in a fog. But in reality, his life was indeed a living hell, deteriorating into nothingness with each passing moment, with each body he sent to the morgue in some disgusting, mangled fashion. Killing beyond the norm was Zack's way of displaying his creativity for all to discover; and he realized that his killing spree couldn't last forever; even that made him angry.

Chapter 49

The police were baffled by July 4, 2000. There were nine bizarre murders in the last year with absolutely no clues or suspects. There were no signs of struggle at any of the crime scenes. There weren't any apparent break-ins, no fluid samples of any kind, no fingerprints, and no suspects. The police didn't even know whether to classify them as related. The only things similar about all of the victims were that someone was unbelievably angry at them and they were all killed outrageously, save for the cab driver, who simply had his throat gouged. There was little anyone could do, and this upset Detective Pinson, who was reading the paper naked sitting Indian style on the floor of Zack's apartment while he massaged her shoulders.

Zack had desperately wanted to spend the holiday with Victoria, but she was once again in the Caribbean with her fiancé. She had informed Zack in late June that not only was she engaged but also that she was pregnant, and he then hit rock bottom, not leaving the apartment other than for work for another two weeks. Heather was the only woman other than his mother who didn't piss Zack off. So he spent time with her to have something to do. He liked her, and she liked him. But he could sense that she was beginning to really like him in a more serious vein. And no matter what, Zack loved Victoria and was still trying to figure out a way to convince her to be with him. He didn't care that she was going to have someone else's child or be hitched.

Heather could sense that their feelings didn't quite match up, but she kept her head up and even told Zack that in a different time and place they could be more serious. Zack agreed. She was a tough cop. As emotionally mismatched as they were, they spent the entire day and night together, and watched the fireworks snuggled on the futon.

Chapter 50

"Grandma Lucille has lung cancer," Dorothy told Zack plainly, and then she broke down. Zack didn't know what to do. He took a couple of personal days and flew to Texas (the conventional way, with some airline miles) to see his beloved grandmother. His parents picked him up from the airport, and they went directly to the hospital.

"Oh Zachary, my baby," Lucille cried out as a tearful Zack ran to the bed and gave her the biggest hug and kiss he ever had. "It's so good to see you, baby! Did you leave work to come here?"

"Of course, Grandma," Zack said. "I had to come see how you're feeling."

"It hurts," she said with a giggle. Zack laughed with her but then teared up even more. His parents left the room. "You know, Zack, I can tell you're in some kind of trouble. I'm not going to ask you what you've been doing. But listen to me now. You have to get yourself together." Zack just stared at her.

She continued: "I remember when you were a teenager and your father told the story about how he was in the Army and was the only black man in the regiment. He had to stay in his own barracks, even though he was supposed to be a part of the team. You were so upset you ran out of the room. I had never seen you that angry. I didn't even know what to say to you. So I left you alone. And now I think I should have said something. You look today just like you did that afternoon, way back when. I don't want you to say anything. Just promise me something." Zack nodded. "Whatever it is that's bothering you, keep remembering that all the things your parents and your grandfather and I, and our parents, and their parents as slaves, went through, we went through it so that eventually someone in the family wouldn't have to. You don't have to, Zachary. Now we know how people can be, and just because laws changed don't mean nothing. Most people are going to act just like their parents or that damn television you love teaches them to act. You just worry about yourself and get yourself a family that you can take care of to get your mind off these people you can't do anything about. Will you promise me that?" Zack promised. "And don't you think this is some final speech I'm giving you, either. I just got diagnosed with this cancer stuff. I'm gonna be around much longer, so I'll be keeping my eye on you, baby. Now go on and help your folks. They're more worried than I am!" She gave Zack a kiss and sent him on his way.

With a stunned look, Zack walked out of the hospital room, and he and his parents went home to have some barbecue and catch up. Grandma was

OK for now, but she knew that Zack wasn't; and Zack knew that his behavior had to change.

Chapter 51

Cousin Benny finally came up to New York to visit Zack on August 12, a sunny Saturday afternoon. Zack and Benny shared a huge, long hug. Their knees hit each other in the process. Zack's knee was just about recovered from the Tribeca fiasco during which he slipped in the pool of blood, and now it would hurt again for a while.

Benny lived in Dallas and, in one of the great ironies of Zack's life, was one of the better young criminal lawyers in the state of Texas. He had been a mailman in a past life. Benny had been working nonstop for nearly two years and had seen Zack only at Christmas-time, when Zack would go back to visit everyone. So it had been a couple of years since they had seen each other. He stopped in for the day on the way home from a trial in Boston. Party time.

"Oh man, this is great," Benny yelled after the third of the pair's whiskey shots. "Zack, I can't believe this damn job has been keeping me from this good ole' drinking and skirt chasing we used to do. Today, we're gonna make up for it!"

"Word!" Zack yelled back to him, signaling to the bartender for another round of beers. They were hanging out at an East Village pub known for being only marginally crowded during the weekend days. That way, they could catch up, watch the games, flirt with women who came in, and seduce the bartender, male or female, into buying back drinks for them. They already had checked in with the fellas up at Maurice's earlier in the day and were now alone.

"So what's been up, my man," Benny said, grabbing Zack's shoulder like longtime friends do. "You stayin' outta trouble? I don't want to have to prosecute you. And I'll do it, nigga!" Big laughter erupted from both of them.

"Man please, you know I'm the choir boy virgin," Zack replied between chuckles. "I don't do anything wrong until you show up. So don't test me, and you better watch out for my liquor intake, too!"

The two finished in the East Village and decided to take a cab up to the Upper West Side to another place Zack knew of. The first cab that appeared scooped them up. "Damn, normally it ain't like that up here," Benny said, laughing. Zack just shook his head and looked out the window, thinking to himself that his actions might have changed the culture within the fraternity that is the New York cab drivers. Or maybe he just scared the shit out of them.

While the pair was walking up Broadway toward the next bar, a group of guys were walking toward them. They were clean cut and looked like they were coming from or going to a wedding for a friend or something. Zack and

Benny got to the bar doors just before the group, and Zack opened the door and Benny went inside. Feeling chivalrous, he held the door open for everyone else. Not one of them said thank you or even looked in his direction. It was as if the door held itself open. Zack didn't say anything. But Benny did.

"Hahahaha, I can see that look on your face. Those white boys just walked in and didn't say shit, did they? Man, you know how it is, they do that shit all the time and don't even know it." Zack's expression didn't change. Benny was right. But Zack was still incensed. He calmed enough to have a few more beers and kept shootin' the breeze. He walked toward the bar. One of the guys who ignored him at the door was in front of him waiting for a beer. He turned around quickly and spilled some beer on Zack's shirt.

"Jesus Christ," Zack yelled.

"Oh, sorry bro," the man replied calmly and kept walking. Zack thought to himself, "I'm not your brother, quit trying to relate to me. You acted like you didn't even fucking see me before." But he held it together.

Zack bought the next round and he slowly moved his conversation with Benny closer to the group of ignoring guys. He overheard them talking about baseball and chimed in. Eventually they were all having a conversation about sports and women. It was the best time Zack and Benny had talking to other men in so long, fraternizing and enjoying life. But Zack had other plans. He asked what they did for a living. Three were professionals, and one was a freelance graphic artist. Benny had to catch the flight home that evening, so the pair went outside to talk for a few more minutes. Benny then told Zack he loved him, gave him a hug, and got in a cab to the airport.

Zack went back inside and hung around until the group of guys called it a night. He followed the one who spilled his beer on him. Once out of the bar, the man had no idea he was even being followed. Zack was invisible, once again. The man lived in the area. Zack quickly darted behind a bush when nobody happened to be around. He chanted and flew back, barely catching a glimpse of the man rounding a corner. Catching up, Buzz followed him into his building and then his apartment on the fourth floor. The man put his keys on the mantle and walked toward the refrigerator. Buzz saw a knife on the counter, chanted, and fell to the floor behind the man, who turned around and screamed, "What the fuck?" Zack grabbed the knife just before him and plunged it into his chest. The man staggered back, rammed into the refrigerator, and fell to the floor, dead with blood pouring out of his mouth and the bottom of his tucked-in shirt filling with blood and sagging sideways.

Without warning, a screaming woman ran from the back of the apartment. Taken completely by surprise, Zack turned and avoided her as she rushed by him, grabbed her in a bear hug from behind, pinning her arms to her sides and lumbered with her over to the open window. She was screaming so loud that people on the street stopped to look up. What they soon saw was a woman flying out of the window and slamming into the concrete sidewalk so hard that her top row of teeth flew 30 feet into the street and were immediately scattered by an oncoming truck. Zack was in a complete panic. He chanted and morphed into Buzz, escaped through the window and flew home as blood seeped out of the woman's head, spreading over the entire sidewalk length. Zack had now killed 11 people.

Chapter 52

Seven months went by, including another autumn and another winter. It was March 2001. Zack was tired. His work wasn't up to standard at the office, and Jim Sheridan gave him a warning about coming in late. Zack had finally listened to his grandmother and stopped killing. But was it too late for redemption? His life had spiraled into a never-ending and vicious cycle of violence that he had come to enjoy so much that he was now miserable every minute of every day. He was turning into Buzz every day, then sneaking into apartment after apartment to watch women shower or have sex; sitting in on private meetings the mayor was having and finding out stunning information he could tell nobody; landing on piles of animal waste and getting into fights with other flies; and even landing on celebrities and enjoying the moment until they felt him and shooed him off. It was the first time that he had ever liked anything to the point of hating himself. He was on the verge of using Buzz to get into women's apartments and then having Zack have his way with them. Misery and fatigue had swallowed him whole. He couldn't sleep any more, and his muscles ached constantly. He had stopped being so violent, but he was still abusing the phenomenon. And he missed the violence, even though he had abandoned it.

The same things that bothered him and pushed him over the edge had not pushed others to the same level. Zack began to believe he was weak and inferior, and that his father would be devastated with embarrassment had he ever known what his son had become. But thoughts of taking his own life never crossed his mind. He just sat in the apartment, watching his sad life go by, waiting for police to arrive that he knew would never come. There was simply no way anyone would ever tie him to the death of anybody. Zack didn't fit the profile. And he had killed a lot of people, 11 in fact. He was a serial killer by definition but not by tradition. The realization was so heavy on his soul that he couldn't even cry any more. He just realized it, and that was it. He had let down Grandma Lucille and couldn't possibly tell her. He knew she was right about everything. He had been raised so well. There was no excuse for his actions. Zack tried to come up with reasons for his dip into ultraviolent behavior, not having any clue that the Everything Bar he forgot about eating while drunk pushed him over the edge.

He began to count the number of times he had been completely looked through or past like he wasn't even there, unless, of course, something was at stake for the other guy. He remembered when a white guy had rolled his window down and spit on the car while his mom was driving to the store with him; he remembered the time he was pulled over and handcuffed by white cops for kidnapping when he was taking a light-skinned black girl home after a date. The cops didn't let him go until they verified that she was not white. When Zack screamed at them, "If she's black, it ain't a kidnapping any more?" they arrested him for disturbing the peace. He remembered the black kids who called him white because he did well in school. He remembered the white kids who called him white because he did well in school. He remembered the white people in college who constantly asked him what sport he was there to play. He remembered the time the Mexican coach at the high school in Texas said, "Alright! Affirmative Action is alive and well," when Zack showed up to interview him on his first day as a sportswriter. He remembered visiting his cousins in the ghetto and hearing gunshots and seeing everyone look like they were struggling so much and then feeling bad when he got home to his nicer accommodations. When he got older he realized that no matter where he lived or how he lived, everyone who looked like him was treated the same way. And he remembered the hundreds of times over the years that he was called a nigger, or a spade, or a coon, or a moolie, or a darkie. He had lots of valuable friendships with people of all races, yet these instances were so etched in his being that he couldn't escape the anger. To Zack, it was unbelievable that every black man in America wasn't a serial killer, and even more stunning that only two or three were ever recorded as such. And to him, that said something very positive about black men and their ability to turn the other cheek after all this bullshit for all these decades and decades. Zack, however, felt like a failure. He was so ashamed that he had stopped calling his parents as often that he cried nightly about it. He was lonely before, but now he was both lonely and alone in spirit. Everyone he knew was there for him, but he was too far gone to allow them to help or to even recognize that they were available to talk to.

The only thing that made him even sadder than his own life was his situation with Victoria. In his mind, Zack was never able to convince her that he was right for her, and he was tired from thinking about it nearly all day and all night. He had so much blood on his hands. And he saw no way out from his woes, so he just gave in to his urges. He knew he was going to hell, so he decided to earn it. He didn't have any money left because he had spent it all on gifts for Victoria. They had gotten closer and closer over time, as she realized she had made a mistake and rid herself of the fiancé. But they had not yet shared the passionate kiss that Zack believed would have changed both of their lives forever.

Bringing his mind back to reality, Zack knew he got paid the next day but had no food left in his apartment. The only thing he could think of was to fly over to the diner across the street and seek crumbs. It was an embarrassing and dignity-reducing decision, but at least only he knew that he was doing it. He left a message for Victoria. He told her that he loved her, as he had before as her best friend, but he tried to make it sound more romantic this time. He had missed her call earlier that day while he was in a meeting. She sounded like she had something important to tell him, which gave him his last bit of hope left. But he had heard it all before, only to be let down, so his excitement was tempered more than ever before. All the money he spent, all the conversations, and all the closeness was not enough. At the end of the day, Victoria was attracted to everything Zack had to offer except Zack himself.

Zack had forgotten the chant, so he got the book out, recited it once again, morphed, and flew over to the diner. Flying around, the restaurant was cleaner than normal, which wasn't good news, seeing as though Buzz was starving. But in the corner booth was a family, and they were eating a lot of food. It was a couple and their son, who looked to be about five years old, maybe six. He was in the corner of the booth, so Buzz thought maybe he could fly around the parents and rest comfortably near the edge of the table and crawl up slowly to the bread crumbs that were near the young boy. In his experience, kids never really cared about flies being around. He hovered a bit and then rested on the table.

The couple was talking about money and they were into it. The boy was paying attention to his action figure and just finished his water. Buzz crawled slowly to one of the crumbs and started munching on it. It was so good, he thought. He knew he would be paid tomorrow and be able to go to the grocery store and stock up, but tonight he just needed a bit of food to get him through. The parents were still discussing money and laughing, paying no attention to their son. Buzz was comfortable. On the verge of biting into the last bit of bread crumb remaining, he heard a loud thud all around him. Startled, he looked around and realized that he was surrounded by glass. Disoriented, he heard the muffled sounds of the couple grabbing the young boy playfully and leaving the table. The boy had turned his glass upside down and caught Buzz in it, trapping him on the table. He tried to say the chant, but he didn't get it right. He had just used it, but it had been so long that he forgot it again quickly; and coming close wasn't good enough. Buzz couldn't believe it! He kept trying to get it right. He figured someone would come and clean the table shortly and pull the glass away and he'd fly off. But nobody came for several minutes. The air was nonexistent and Buzz began to panic and start to feel faint. He flipped over on his back and was starting to hallucinate and lose his breath. Someone was coming, but they were so far away. He had tried several variations of the chant. None were exactly right. His breath had become so short that he knew he was running out of time. He cried out so loudly to the ears of nobody, sobbing for his parents and his friends.

His helplessness heard by no one, Buzz breathed his last exhalation at the exact moment that the dishwasher picked the glass up off of the table. Buzz was unconscious. The dishwasher wiped him into the bin with the other dishes from the table and walked quickly to the back behind the kitchen. The scalding hot water was already running and Buzz was about 10 seconds from being washed away. He was seeing white light at the time and could feel nothing. He saw images of his family smiling, Victoria reaching out to him, and an image of a large being without shape that felt welcoming. He hoped it would be God but knew that it had more of a chance of being Satan. The white light disappeared. Buzz was dead. The dishwasher wiped him and the dishes into the waiting water, and his limp, fly body floated unnoticed in the sudsy water for a few minutes and then spiraled down the drain. He flowed through the pipes underneath the diner, and slowly bobbed and weaved around trash, human waste, and other chemicals and carriers of dirt to the sewer system, and then out to sea. Buzz, aka Zack Williams, possibly the most confused, lonely, twisted, charismatic, angry, witty, decent, and tormented serial killer in American history, was gone.

Chapter 53

Detectives Julian Wright and Heather Pilson arrived at Zack's apartment a week later, seeking clues to his disappearance. They were allowed to investigate because they had spoken with Zack after the Jackson murder. Zack's parents and the human resources department of the Executive Publisher had filed missing person's reports. Wright and Pilson put on their gloves, but they found nothing that would be of interest to anyone or anything out of the ordinary. It never occurred to them to check the floor for any amounts of blood residue from his victims, because he was never a suspect in any of the cases and was only indirectly tied to one of them, the Jackson murder.

Wright saw the Indian book on the table but thought nothing of it, of course. Heather did a great job of acting like she had never been there before, checking the drawers she had already been familiar with. She opened the drawer where she had gotten the t-shirt she slept in. The one she borrowed was on top. It took everything inside her to hold it together. But she managed to keep her professionalism. The apartment was dusty, so Wright pulled back the television stand. There were dozens of wires stacked on top of each other, a pair of scissors and a sports almanac on the floor. He then went over to the futon and pulled it from the wall it was up against. Tons of dust had built up behind it. There was something sticking out of the dust. Wright picked it up. It was a plastic soda bottle. Wright dusted it off. It was the soda bottle Zack had bought nearly two years ago at the bodega. It still had the candy wrapper Zack stuffed into it. Wright opened the bottle and recoiled at the scent that stormed out. He immediately screwed the cap back on and told Heather that he was going to give the bottle to forensics. He put the bottle in an evidence bag he pulled out of his suit pocket and told Heather he was going to have a cigarette. Heather said she'd be there in a second and wanted to check the bathroom. On her way, she saw Zack's cell phone on the dresser. When she opened it, the phone display read that there were several voicemail messages. She pushed the button for voicemail and waited. The first message was from Dorothy. Heather erased it quickly, not wanting to hear the tragic words that would never be returned. The next message was from Ron, then Stevie, Cousin Benny, Dorothy and Robert, Martha, his parents again, and the last one was from Victoria. Heather, not thinking about the fact that one of the calls could give a clue to Zack's disappearance, erased all of the other messages quickly, but decided to listen to the last one.

Victoria was despondent and said, "Hi baby, it's me, Vic. I've had more than enough time to think about things, and I've been so blind. But now I am ready to do what I should have done a long time ago. And that is to snatch you up. I can't begin to tell you what you mean to me, and I know this will make you smile. I don't just love you, I am in love with you and all of the good things you've done for me. Call me back, or better yet, just come over. I'll be here waiting." Heather closed the phone and walked into the restroom, closed the door, sat on the closed toilet seat, and cried softly into her hands. To her left, hanging from the shower curtain rod, was the speed skating outfit.

Wright got a call from forensics at midnight. The wrapper inside the bottle found at Zack's apartment contained trace amounts of a toxic substance the department couldn't immediately identify, as well as cocaine, saliva, and other chemical elements linked to the common housefly. Confused, Wright hung up and had no idea how this information would help him figure out where Zack was. For weeks on end, Zack's family and friends held out hope that he would return and explain himself. But nothing materialized. Six months later, the authorities in New York had made the decision to close the book on Zack.

When Jim Sheridan announced to Zack's colleagues that he was presumed dead and the case was closed, there was a silence that was different from the norm. Nobody looked directly at one another, and Martha's whimpering cries were the only thing that could be faintly heard behind her closed door.

Police slowly walked toward Dorothy and Robert's home in Dallas, and upon telling them the news from New York, Dorothy fell straight to the floor, kicking and screaming, and Robert, sobbing, held her, stroking her face and saying, over and over, "Oh son, where are you? Where are you, son? Where are you?" He repeated it more than 50 times. Despite Zack having been gone for months already, their collective screams were so loud that neighbors called the police from four different homes nearby.

Zack's friends and acquaintances from all over the country, many of which he hadn't spoken with at all since he started his descent, were stunned and the mood never returned to the way it had been in many of their lives. In his torment and debilitating anger, Zack may never have known what he meant to each of them.

Victoria received a call from Wright, who was informing everyone in Zack's rolodex of his status. He called because Heather said she had to leave for a commitment she had forgotten about right when she was asked to make the call. She couldn't do it. Wright told Victoria that Zack was presumed dead. Victoria didn't say a word. She was on her couch, and her daughter was climbing all over her. One lonely tear streaked down her face. It was clear that she might never recover from the realization that she would never see Zack again after finally realizing that he was the one.

The forensic pathologist determined that, since the only evidence in the apartment that could be tested was found to have poisonous elements, the case was officially ruled a homicide. Wright then was finally obligated to make the phone call to Rossage, Montana, to discuss with the authorities a certain Apache Foods, maker of the Everything Bar that was inside the toxic wrapper he found. As expected, Wright had a lengthy conversation with Sheriff Chris David.

Chapter 54

Sheriff David walked slowly toward Daniel Smith's office at Apache Foods. He left Deputy Farley in the car. Daniel warmly greeted the sheriff, who sat down and took off his hat. Daniel could tell that David had something serious to tell him, so he had his secretary hold his calls and he closed the door and sat down at his desk. Farley waited as the two spoke for several minutes, then Daniel closed the door slowly as David walked out and back to the squad car. He got in, started the car, and drove off, saying nothing to Farley as the deputy sat still, looking straight ahead.

Daniel decided not to immediately tell Edmund any of what the sheriff told him. Edmund's condition was a bit worse than it had been, so he was now limited to helping Daniel and his mother, Anna, with some domestic chores and giving small bits of advice on the business end when needed. He no longer worked in the office location and was primarily at home. Daniel made a call to the quality control technician who replaced Greg Farber and asked him if they were still using the same machinery to make the Everything Bar that they had always used. The QCT informed Daniel that they were indeed using the same machines, except that the one that previously had dispensed the pretzel ingredient had been removed from the line by orders of Edmund before the QCT arrived at Apache. The machine was still in a back room. Daniel immediately had it tested at one of the on-site labs. It tested positive for trace amounts of a very toxic poisonous liquid, cocaine residue, and heroin.

Daniel was absolutely stunned by this news. He immediately watched tapes of the mornings around the time when the incident would have happened. He couldn't find anything abnormal on the assembly line during the day shift, which was the only one used for the Everything Bar until it went into mass production. The tapes recorded everything between 6 a.m. and 6 p.m. every day, covering the full- and part-time shifts. He called to ask Al, the night watchman, if he had noticed anything out of the ordinary. Al said, "Not at all, Mr. Smith, but there was a time when Mr. Farber came in mighty early, around 5:45 a.m., if I can recall. Not sure why, but at the time it didn't seem like a big deal, since sometimes people would come in and relax in the cafeteria or something." Daniel thanked him and hung up, burying his head in his hands. He then called Sheriff David to ask him if he was certain he didn't find anything at the scene when he found Greg's body. David told him they didn't find anything out of the ordinary, but he remembered that he allowed Farley to head the scene inspection because it was apparently a random suicide. Thinking he better check again, David went back to Farber's house alone. He found in Greg's closet the long shoe box with all of the tools for destruction wrapped in the lab coat.

At the remote reservation, Great Bear gathered his tribal members around him. He began to tell a story of a dream he had the night before that someone had used one of the many Indian potions they held so sacred as a weapon of evil. The other members knew that it was a story meant to parallel the experience of the man who had come to them a couple of years earlier, Greg Farber. After a prayer, Great Bear excused everyone from the main teepee. The reservation was far away from civilization. But the news of what had happened had reached Great Bear, nonetheless. It took so long for them to find out because Greg had killed himself before the gods could punish him for using the potion for evil. There had been no sign given by the gods to Great Bear, as a result. Had there not been this loophole, of sorts, in the protocol of the gods, or had Great Bear been informed of Greg's suicide before the two-day deadline, he would have been able to, as the oldest member and leader of the tribe, utilize an emergency chant. The chant would have lifted the effects of the potion from the unsuspecting victim, Zack Williams. Great Bear was sworn to secrecy with regard to his ability to serve as a human antidote. And now it was too late. When told that someone far away in New York had consumed what was believed to be the potion, Great Bear put his head down and cried, saying numerous Indian prayers of apology and regret at having allowed Bill Freeman to escape the tribe with the secret chants and for mistakenly blessing and contributing to the potion Greg had brought to him under the cover of his lies. None of this was truly Great Bear's fault, and even though the chances were incredibly small that someone would both see Freeman's chants and ingest the potion who was not an Indian, it happened. He felt so responsible that he stepped down from his position as tribal leader and didn't speak or hold commune with the other members for the rest of his life.

Chapter 55

Sheriff David drove alone to Daniel Smith's residence to give him the sobering news that he had found a box full of incriminating evidence implicating Greg Farber in a sabotage of the pretzel mechanism for the Everything Bar at Apache Foods.

Daniel answered the front door with a grim look on his face and the two spoke for several minutes. David didn't go inside. He told Daniel that not only did he find the items in Greg's closet but that he also had to tell him more information about the tainted candy bar. Daniel's eyes glazed over as David told him that the wrapper was not just found in a New York City apartment, as he had told him before. It just so happened that the man who lived there and presumably ate the tainted bar disappeared six months prior and had been questioned in two murder cases, though he wasn't a suspect. They finished talking, shook hands, and then David returned to his car with his head down.

Daniel then walked down his hallway and into his living room. It took forever to get there, it seemed. He picked up the newspaper out of his chair and sat down with it in his lap next to the fireplace, trying to figure out a way to tell his dearest friend Edmund what happened. He could not envision a darker day in his life, not since he was a very young boy and had been called a name at the hardware store. He decided to give Edmund the rest of the day off so he could think about what to do. A proud, patriotic, and purposeful man of substance, Daniel Smith had no idea how life could be any worse for him at the moment. Tears welled in his eyes. Before he called Edmund in the room, Daniel stared straight ahead, his hands folded on top of his paper. It was the national edition of *The New York Times*, dated Sept. 10, 2001.

About the Author

S.L. Freeman was born in New York City in 1966 and has lived in Texas, Illinois, and Washington, D.C. A graduate of Texas A&M University, he is an author, advertising professional, and webmaster, and was one of three African-American newspaper sports editors in the country in the early 1990s in Texas. He currently lives in New York City.

An ancient Indian potion and a man on the edge of insanity meet, with horrifying results, in S.L. Freeman's satirical, socially thought-provoking, and hard-hitting look at a city dweller driven to the brink. Read between the lines and find out if you have anything in common with…

Buzz

ISBN 978-0-6151-8397-8

ID: 1705703
www.lulu.com